P9-EDF-220

⟨12⟩

THE GIRLS OF CANBY HALL

WHO'S THE NEW GIRL?

EMILY CHASE

SCHOLASTIC INC.

New York Toronto London Auckland Sydney Tokyo

ISBN 0-590-33472-7

12 11 10 9 8 7 6 5 4 3 2 1   4   5 6 7 8 9/8 0/9

Printed in the U.S.A.

THE GIRLS
OF CANBY HALL

WHO'S THE
NEW GIRL?

THE GIRLS
OF CANBY HALL

CHAPTER ONE

I've had it!" Dana Morrison announced, tossing her snow-covered parka on the floor of her dormitory room. "It's practically a blizzard out there. Look at me! I've ruined my hair, my new Italian boots just fell apart — and I'm a total mess!"

"You said it, girl." Faith Thompson looked at her roommate and couldn't help smiling. There was something funny about someone as sophisticated as Dana getting caught in a snowstorm — that was the sort of thing that should only happen to other people! In all the time that she and Dana and Shelley Hyde had shared a room in Baker House, she had never seen Dana look anything less than perfect.

But at the moment, Dana Morrison — bright, beautiful, and New York-hip — looked as miserable as a wet kitten. She had made the mile-long trek into Greenleaf — the nearest town to Canby Hall — for sup-

1

plies, and the blizzard had caught her by surprise on the way back. She peeled off her soggy jeans and groped in the closet for her white terry robe — the thick, luxurious one her mother had brought back from a buying trip to Paris.

"Well, you don't have to agree with me," she said, giving a gigantic sneeze. "I've been staggering through snowdrifts like I was Admiral Byrd, and this is the thanks I get."

"That's what friends are for," Faith teased. "I just hope you remembered to get me pretzels." She laughed and eased her lanky frame off her studio bed to study Dana.

"I got you pretzels, and Twinkies for Shelley, and nachos, and peanuts, and —" She had to stop to sneeze again, and Faith handed her a box of Kleenex.

"You know, Dana, I have to admit, I kind of like you this way," she said. "Wet hair, streaky makeup, runny nose . . . at least it shows you're human. Isn't that right, Shel?"

"Absolutely," Shelley Hyde piped up from behind her French book. "It's nice to know that even Dana Morrison can get a red nose like everyone else." Shelley was the third roommate in 407 Baker House, and she giggled as she bounced off the bed to plug in the hot plate. "You know, when I first met you, Dana, I thought you were so perfect you never had a split end!"

Faith ran a hand through her curly Afro,

and said, "Yeah, we figured you were one of those high-fashioned types who sleep in orange lip gloss!" She settled back down on the floor mattress with a bag of pretzels. At the beginning of the school year, the girls in 407 had put their bed frames in storage and made studio couches out of their mattresses. Each girl had her own ideas on decorating, and Faith had chosen a wild batik print for a bedspread, topped with a jumble of throw pillows.

Dana blew her nose and managed a rueful smile. "Enough, you two. You shouldn't make fun of someone who's coming down with double pneumonia. I can't believe it. The radio said snow flurries. What a joke!" She shook some snow out of her tangled brown hair and debated whether or not she should blow it dry. *Why bother?* she decided. She had no intention of going out again tonight for anything! "The least you can do is get me a cup of whatever it is you're drinking," she added. "I'm so cold, my teeth are chattering."

"Would you believe diet cocoa?" Faith grimaced. "It's one of Shelley's concoctions."

"Hey, you said it wasn't bad," Shelley protested.

"It's not bad, but it doesn't taste like cocoa." Faith winked at Dana, who had finished drying herself off and was hunting for a pair of giant furry slippers.

"You just have to use your imagination,

that's all. In case you're wondering, those little lumpy things are dehydrated marshmallows." Shelley Hyde carefully poured out two mugs of cocoa and handed one to Dana. Even in the bulky robe, with her hair tucked into a striped towel, Dana still looked glamorous, she thought. And thin! Shelley had battled her weight ever since she could remember, although she had certainly slimmed down since she had come to Canby Hall. She had been very chubby during her first few weeks at the Massachusetts boarding school. All that country cooking that her mother did in Pine Bluff, Iowa, had added on the pounds, and she flinched when she looked at snapshots taken during Orientation Week. She looked "corn-fed;" there was no other word for it, she decided. With her round face, curly blonde hair, and dimples, she could have been a teenage Shirley Temple!

But luckily, the food at Canby Hall took away your appetite, she thought wryly. And now she had a terrific incentive to watch her weight — she had three new pairs of designer jeans hanging in her closet. She sipped her cocoa and looked outside. Even though it was barely five in the afternoon, the January sky was already turning dark, and a fierce wind was rattling the windows. "Shouldn't we head over to the dining hall now? If we wait until six, it'll be a mob scene."

"I know. It always amazes me that people

would stand in line for spinach surprise," Dana said, tucking her robe around her, and drawing her knees up to her chest. "But I'm going to pass, tonight. I can't face going out again. And I especially can't face the dining hall." She took a sip of cocoa and made a face. "Shelley, what did you put in this?"

"You don't want to know," Faith interjected.

"Well, at least it's low-calorie," Shelley said defensively. "Doesn't anybody want to go to dinner with me? How about you, Faith?" She had only eaten a salad for lunch, and her stomach gave a warning rumble.

"Count me out, Shel. It's Tuesday, and that means it's Mystery Stew night."

"Oh no, I forgot," Shelley groaned. The Canby Hall cook was into recycling, and Monday night's leftovers appeared in barely disguised form on Tuesday night.

"Let's stay in tonight," Dana suggested, snuggling under a quilt on her floor mattress. "You know it's kind of cozy, with the wind howling against the windows, and us safe and warm inside."

"And our stomachs all growling in tune . . ." Shelley muttered. Maybe it was because she was raised on a farm, but Shelley could never get used to Dana and Faith's big-city habits of skipping meals and snacking. To her, dinner would always mean meat, potatoes, vegetables, and dessert!

"I've got potato chips, crackers, and peanut butter," Dana offered. "We could survive on that tonight."

"You could probably survive on anything," Shelley said. "I don't think you eat more than eight hundred calories a day, anyway."

"Well, I've got to starve myself to fit into the samples," Dana laughed. "Although sometimes I practically need a shoe horn to do it." Dana's mother worked as a buyer for a New York department store, and kept her supplied with the latest fashions. A lot of the "sample" clothes were given away once a promotion was over, and Dana usually got them. The trouble was, they were invariably size six, which meant that she needed to be bone-thin to wear them.

"You know, it must be nice to have a mother who's a buyer," Faith said thoughtfully. "Sometimes I think all my mother brings home are headaches, instead of presents."

"Maybe that's because she gets so involved with her clients, and wants to help them," Shelley suggested. She had met Faith's mother, who was a social worker, on a visit to Washington, D.C., and liked her very much. It hadn't been easy for Faith's mother to send her to Canby Hall. Faith's father was a police officer who had been killed in the line of duty, and there were two other children in the family as well. But Mrs. Thompson wanted

Faith to have the best education possible, and Faith was determined to study hard and not let her down.

It wasn't easy for Faith being the only black girl at Canby Hall, either. There had been some rough times before the girls in 407 accepted the fact that they came from very different backgrounds. Faith and Dana were both big-city girls, streetwise and smart, with an opinion on everything. Shelley was from a different world completely — she was a country girl from Iowa who wanted to be an actress more than anything in the world. Somehow the girls had worked out their differences after a few initial misunderstandings, and had become fast friends.

"I've got an idea," Faith said suddenly. "It's too cold and depressing to go to the dining hall, so why don't we have a picnic right here, and invite Alison?"

"Or better yet, let's bring the food up to her! She's got more room than we do." Shelley grinned and started gathering up the snacks.

"Hey, wait a minute, you two," Dana protested. "How can I go anywhere looking like this? At least let me dry my hair and put on some eye makeup."

"No way," Shelley said. "Join the crowd and look awful once in a while." She turned and grinned at her roommate. "It will keep you humble."

A few minutes later, a surprised Alison

Cavanaugh opened the door to a chorus of giggles. Her job as housemother at Baker House had taught her to expect the unexpected, especially from the girls she called "The Three Musketeers."

"It's chow time," Dana announced, cheerfully waving a bag of potato chips and a six-pack of Tab. Faith and Shelley brought up the rear, carrying paper bags of cheese, crackers, and corn chips.

"What's this — a toga party?" Alison asked laughingly. She stared at Dana, who was still draped in a robe and had a towel around her head.

"No, this is what happens when you battle the sleet and snow and make a food run for your friends — who don't appreciate it," she added, pretending to glare at Shelley and Faith.

"Well, come in and tell me what's going on," Alison said, ushering them into her apartment on the top floor of Baker House, affectionately known as "The Penthouse." Alison had made it one of the coziest rooms the girls had ever seen by scattering some oversized pillows on the wood floors, and covering the windows with creamcolored, gauzy curtains. There were dozens of green plants, and a whole wall lined with bookcases. It was a place for fun, laughter, and confidences, which Alison shared constantly with her "girls" at Canby Hall.

"We've all decided to boycott the dining hall tonight," Faith explained, spreading out a junk food feast on Alison's coffee table, "and we thought maybe you'd like to join us. It's Mystery Stew night," she added, in case Alison needed any encouragement.

"I'd love it," Alison exclaimed. "You saved me from opening a can of soup, and curling up with a book I didn't want to read anyway." She glanced at the selection of junk food. "But let's make one small change. Let me rustle up a giant pot of chili for us, okay? We can have the . . . uh . . . snacks on the side."

"You're on!" Shelley said enthusiastically. She looked at Alison admiringly. Sometimes it was hard to think of Alison as a housemother. She was so hip and laid-back, she was more like a best friend. On this particular night, she was wearing one of her favorite outfits, a beaded Indian skirt, and a cotton top that had dozens of tiny mirrors sewn onto it. Her thick hair was as wild and untamable as ever — it was a reddish-brown color, and cascaded around her shoulders. She was young, just twenty-six years old, and as far as the girls in 407 were concerned, she was one of the most terrific people on campus.

"Well, come on," she said, waving her arm, and setting a bunch of thin silver bracelets jangling, "let's head for the kitchen."

"How fast can you make chili from scratch?" Faith asked. "We're starving."

"Really fast," Alison said. "In one pot, too. As soon as the ground beef browns, we're going to throw in some tomato soup and chili pepper and beans, and voila! Instant chili. Well, not exactly instant," she amended. "We need to let the whole thing simmer for ten minutes. I spent a summer in Texas," she went on, "and I had a . . . friend . . . who was a chili nut. He even entered chili cooking contests, can you imagine?"

"Alison," Shelley teased her, "you never told us you had a romance with a tall, handsome Texan!"

"How did you guess he was tall and handsome?" Alison countered in mock surprise.

"I bet she never told Michael, either," Faith added. Michael Frank was the guidance counselor at Canby Hall, and he and Alison had been dating for several months.

"Even a housemother has to have some secrets," Alison said, smiling at Faith. "You think that you girls have all the romantic problems. Well, believe me," she said grinning, "it just isn't so." A few minutes later, she dished out the chili in earthenware bowls, added crackers and French bread, and arranged everything on the living room table. "Dig in, gang," she said, settling herself on the floor.

There was a contented silence while everyone sampled the chili and pronounced it the best they had ever eaten.

"I think it could have cooked a little longer," Alison said. "But I knew it would hit the spot on a night like this." As soon as the words were out, a giant gust of wind rattled the skylight, and Alison flinched. "What a night," she muttered. "And to think we've got another couple of months of it."

"It would be fun to go someplace, wouldn't it?" Dana said thoughtfully, wandering over to the window. The Canby Hall campus was blanketed in snow, and she could see a couple of girls making a mad dash for the front porch of Baker House.

"Like where?" Faith said absently. "I hate to say it, but my hometown is a pile of slush at the moment. And New York is out — that's just more of the same."

"We even get snow in Iowa," Shelley offered. "Not that I figured anybody was panting to go there," she added, when everyone looked at her in surprise.

"I'm afraid everything in the whole Northeast is bad news in January," Alison said slowly.

"Then let's try the Southeast," Dana spoke up.

"What?" Alison asked blankly.

"The Southeast. Like . . . Florida. Yes, Florida," she said, speaking quickly. "Why don't we go to Florida over semester break?"

"It would sure beat hanging around the campus," Faith said, her face breaking into a big smile. "Florida! Dana, I have to admit that every once in a while, you come up with a winner."

"Would it work?" Shelley asked. "I mean, could we really go? How would we get there? Where would we stay?"

"I don't know," Alison said. She cupped her chin in her hand and looked thoughtful.

"Those are minor details," Dana said excitedly. "We can work all that out later. It's not such a wild idea, you know. A lot of schools encourage their kids to travel over break. Alison, you could be our chaperone. You and Michael."

A little smile played around Alison's lips, and she shook her head reprovingly. "You really know how to get to me, don't you? Well, let me think about it," she said with a smile. "And let me talk to P.A. about it. I don't know how thrilled she'd be with the idea. It's a lot of responsibility taking a bunch of girls to Florida." Patrice Allardyce, or "P.A.," was the headmistress at Canby Hall. Ms. Allardyce was very cool and reserved, and the girls found her intimidating at times, but they respected her.

"Even girls as bright and responsible as Canby Hall girls?" Dana said. "After all, P.A. was just saying in assembly last week that she wanted us to be more mature, and to take more control of our lives."

Alison laughed. "I think our esteemed

headmistress was referring to keeping your rooms clean, Dana."

"Oh really?" Dana said innocently. "I didn't get that impression at all. I thought she wanted us to broaden our horizons."

"We could broaden them in Fort Lauderdale," Faith offered. "My sister Sarah went there on spring break with her class at Georgetown, and they had a terrific time. You wouldn't believe some of the stories. . . ." She stopped abruptly when she caught Alison's look. "I mean, it was really an . . . educational experience," she finished with a giggle.

"I'll bet," Alison said wryly, and everyone burst out laughing.

"But seriously, Alison, could we go? Is there even a chance?" Dana persisted. "It would be so fantastic."

"It would be kind of fun," Alison admitted. She ran a hand through her thick hair and sighed. "I really like Fort Lauderdale," she said dreamily. "Moonlit walks on the beach, surfing in the ocean, long afternoons lying around the pool. . . ."

"You left out the best part," Dana said very seriously.

"What's that?"

Dana smiled. "Boys."

"Okay, guys, I'll talk to P.A. tomorrow," Alison said. She paused and grinned at Dana. "And I'm going to pretend you didn't make that last comment. Just remember, if this trip goes, it will have to be educational. Remember that, educational," she said, stressing each syllable.

"Oh, it will be," Dana said seriously. "Fort Lauderdale during semester break will be very educational." She looked at her friends. "Isn't that right, gang?"

"Oh, absolutely," Faith said. "Educational. Like something out of a textbook."

"It will be so educational, we should probably get academic credit for it," Shelley said, dissolving into laughter.

"And get a grade on it," Dana said, playing along with the joke. "Do you think P.A. will go along with a class called 'Boys 101'?"

"I think we better call it a night," Alison said firmly, standing up. She smiled and shook her head. "I've got to be clear-headed when I talk to P.A. tomorrow." She started to clean off the table, and then stopped. "Boys 101, indeed! If P.A. ever heard that, she'd have a fit. I'm going to forget the last ten minutes of this conversation," she said, pretending to be stern.

"Whatever you say, Alison," Dana told her. "Just be as convincing as you can tomorrow. Remember, Fort Lauderdale would be educational for us," she giggled.

"A cultural experience," Faith added.

"It will develop our minds," Shelley said solemnly, as Alison laughed and said goodnight.

CHAPTER TWO

Shelley was still bubbling with excitement the next morning at breakfast. She and her two roommates were sitting with Casey Flint in the dining hall, and the bright winter sunlight streamed in the windows, cutting a path along the heavy oak table. Shelley was busily filling Casey in on the "Florida Project" and Casey's blue eyes were wide with surprise.

"Alison's actually going to do it?" she said incredulously. "She's really going to ask P.A. if she and Michael can take us to Florida?"

"She promised to ask her today," Shelley said. "What do you think about it? You're going to come with us, aren't you?"

Casey nodded, and brushed a lock of curly blonde hair out of her eyes. "Are you kidding? I wouldn't miss it for the world. My parents are going to be in Europe anyway, and they'll be thrilled to know that I won't be home during break."

Nobody said anything for a minute, and Casey went back to her breakfast. On the surface, Casey Flint didn't have a problem in the world — she was cute, blonde, and had the kind of face that could light up in a grin in two seconds flat. But deep down, she had known her share of disappointments. Her parents were wealthy art dealers who jetted around the globe buying paintings for dealers and museums. Even though they kept an apartment in New York, it was really just a stopping-off place. Most of their time was divided among the art capitals of the world — Paris, London, and Florence. The Flints didn't come to Canby Hall often to see Casey. She tried to pretend it didn't matter, and put up a tough and independent front, refusing to play the "poor little rich girl." But her friends knew the hurt and loneliness she sometimes felt. She dressed in faded jeans and T-shirts and said as little as possible about her trendy parents.

"I can't believe we might go to Fort Lauderdale," Shelley said dreamily. "It sounds like paradise."

"What does?" asked a cool, sarcastic voice. Pamela Young plunked her tray down and slid into the seat next to Shelley. For a moment no one answered her, but she didn't seem discouraged by the lack of enthusiasm.

I wonder why she even bothers to sit with us? She must have a short memory, Dana thought resentfully. Pamela was the daughter of a famous movie star, Yvonne Young, and had done her best to break up the friendship of the girls in 407. The tables had been turned on her, but Dana still shuddered when she thought of all the unhappiness Pamela had caused.

Shelley hesitated, but her naturally good manners wouldn't let her just sit there and not speak to Pamela. "We're trying to get Alison to take us on a class trip over semester break," she said quietly.

"Really?" Pamela's eyes widened with interest. "Why would she want to do that?"

A typical Pamela-type reply, Dana thought wearily. *She can't imagine anyone doing anything nice for anyone else!* "Because she's a terrific person, that's why."

"Oh," Pamela said craftily, a little smile curving her lips. She shrugged and sipped her black coffee. "And where is this little . . . expedition going to?"

"Fort Lauderdale!" Shelley blurted out. She hadn't meant to sound enthusiastic around Pamela, who had a way of always making her feel silly, but she couldn't help it. Going to Florida would be just about the most terrific thing she could think of, and she was never any good at hiding her feelings.

"Fort Lauderdale?" Pamela said it disdainfully, as if it were the Black Hole of Calcutta.

"Yes, Fort Lauderdale," Dana said defensively. "You've heard of it, haven't you, Pamela? Sandy beaches and miles of ocean?"

"I've heard of it," she said lightly. "But isn't it rather . . . *outré?*"

"*Outré?*" Pamela had a maddening habit of using French when she wanted to annoy people.

"Out of it," Pamela said shortly. "*Nobody* goes to Fort Lauderdale anymore. Everyone goes to St. Croix, or maybe Andros — that's in the Bahamas," she added patronizingly. "Or if you insist on going to Florida, at least make it the Keys. But Fort Lauderdale!" she laughed, showing her even, white teeth. "I can't believe you're serious. The only people who go there are a bunch of over-age greasers who saw all those Annette Funicello movies."

"Thanks for making our day," Dana said under her breath. She looked at Casey and rolled her eyes. At least there was no danger of Pamela tagging along to Fort Lauderdale with them.

A few seconds later, though, her hopes were dashed. Pamela fingered the solid gold cube she wore around her neck, and said thoughtfully, "You know, it just might be kind of a kick to go to Fort Lauderdale after all. Sort of camp, you know? I mean, I haven't been there since I was practically a baby, and it would be fun to see how things have changed. When did you say the trip was going?"

"It's not definite yet," Faith said quickly.

"Anyway, aren't you going to some place fashionable with your mother over break?" She put just enough emphasis on the word fashionable for Pamela to know that she could be sarcastic, too.

"Well, we were going to Montreal," Pamela drawled. "But you know what? Yvonne got this simply fantastic movie deal in London last week, so she'll be on location for the next couple of months."

"Pity," Casey said, with a touch of an English accent. She looked at Shelley, who smothered a giggle.

"Yes, it is," Pamela said sweetly. "But every cloud has a silver lining, doesn't it? Because now I can go to Fort Lauderdale." She finished her coffee, and pushed away her untouched breakfast. "Honestly, I don't know why they can't get a decent chef in this place. This food is simply unfit for human consumption. Whoever made these eggs must be related to the Borgias."

"Sometimes I wonder if there's anything about Canby Hall that you like," Faith said, looking at her steadily.

"Not much," Pamela said lightly. "I suppose it's all right if you've never been anywhere else." She stood up and Faith noticed that she was wearing one of her favorite "Rodeo Drive" outfits — a creamy suede jumpsuit with Navaho jewelry. Pamela always made an effort to dress differently from

the other girls at Canby Hall, and didn't
have a cardigan sweater or a pair of cords in
her entire wardrobe. "It's kind of like Fort
Lauderdale," she went on. "It's fine, if you've
never been to St. Tropez." She shrugged into
a rabbit fur jacket, tossed her gleaming
blonde hair over her collar, and pushed back
her chair. "Bye, everybody," she said, flashing
a wide smile.

"I think I'm not hungry after all," Faith
said, after Pamela left.

"Pamela has a way of doing that to you,"
Dana said acidly. "Well, I hate to break this
up, gang, but I'm going to be late for algebra."

Shelley looked at her watch and jumped up.
"And I've got an eight o'clock French class.
Let's go!"

"You don't think she'll really come to
Florida with us, do you?" Shelley said a few
minutes later, as she and Dana trudged along
the icy path to the main building. The Canby
Hall campus was blanketed with snow, and
a chill January wind stung their cheeks.

"Pamela?" Dana asked. "I don't think so. I
think she likes to stir things up, and she
knew we weren't wild over the idea." A sudden gust of wind caught the end of her plaid
muffler, and she made a grab for it. "I can't
wait to hear what P.A. has to say, though. I'm
ready for some sunshine!"

"Me too," Shelley agreed.

Canby Hall, with its stately red brick buildings and tree-lined walks, was never more beautiful than in the winter. It had a graceful elegance that set it apart from the chrome and steel high schools that most of the girls were used to. When Horace Canby founded the school in 1897, he dedicated it to his daughter, Julia, who had died of fever. The beautiful estate, with its farm, stables, skating pond, and maple groves, would have been her inheritance.

The school opened with only thirty girls, but rapidly grew to two hundred and fifty. In the early days, classes were held in the main building, and Baker House was the only dormitory. Since then, the science building and library had been added, plus tennis courts, and a sports center. Many of the girls attended the school on full or partial scholarships, including Faith, Dana and Shelley. All three of them had a special feeling for the school, and felt very lucky to be there.

"See you at lunch," Shelley said, as she and Dana parted company in the hall of the main building. "Maybe there'll be some good news by then."

"Okay, I'll see you at the salad bar at twelve. Have fun in French," Dana teased. Shelley had no ear for foreign languages, and Dana and Faith spent hours drilling her on verbs and idioms.

"You had to say that," Shelley said ruefully. She sighed and walked into her French class, feeling tremendously sorry for herself. It was bad enough to have to take French, but to take it at eight o'clock in the morning was . . . what was that word her teacher always used? *Incroyable!* That was it. Incredible. It was absolutely incredible.

She opened her book and tried to concentrate on the perilous journey of Monsieur Dupont as he made his way through the Paris Metro system. But no matter how hard she tried, her mind kept drifting back to sandy beaches, sunshine, and bikinis. Bikinis! Her mind stopped short. How could she squeeze into a bikini? And it was just a few weeks till semester break. She resolved to live on celery sticks, if necessary.

After all, she knew Dana would be wearing something sensational — probably a French cut tank suit — and she didn't want to look like a blob standing next to her. If Dana wasn't such a good friend, it would be very easy to be jealous of her, Shelley decided. She looked absolutely terrific in everything she put on, and didn't have a worry in the world.

At that very moment, Dana had more worries than Shelley could imagine. Mr. Mitchell, the math teacher, had picked her for "board work," and she was suffering through a tangled quadratic equation. She hated it when she had to work a problem on the board right in front of the whole class. It was like writing your mistakes on a billboard for everyone to see! Of course, she should have spent more time on her homework last night, but the session at Alison's had lasted longer than anyone had expected. And it had been fun, she thought, smiling. A chance to go to Florida with her friends. Fantastic! That's what it would be.

"Remember, in mathematics, everything has to balance," Mr. Mitchell was saying sharply. Dana forced herself back to the real world then, and looked helplessly at the blackboard. "It's very simple, Dana. Everything on the right side has to equal everything on the left side," he said, with just a hint of reproach in his voice.

Easy for you to say! she thought ruefully. Her answer was off by a mile. Dana stared blankly at the numbers, as if she could change them by sheer force of will, like those people who can make forks move across the table, just by concentrating.

"Really, Dana," Mr. Mitchell said sadly, "I don't think your heart is in this."

"Sorry," she muttered. She felt the same way about algebra that Shelley felt about French.

"Let's try someone else for this problem," Mr. Mitchell added heavily. "You can sit down now, Dana."

Dana escaped gratefully to her seat. She felt

a little guilty about letting Mr. Mitchell down — after all, it wasn't his fault that he taught an impossible subject — but how could she concentrate on numbers when her mind was on Florida? She glanced at her watch. Alison had promised to meet them for lunch and let them know what P.A. had decided . . . and that was exactly three hours and forty-five minutes away. *I'd give anything to hear the conversation between P.A. and Alison,* she thought. *Alison — please be as persuasive as you can!* she added silently.

At that moment, Alison was being very persuasive. At least that's the way it looked to Faith from behind a giant potted fern. She wasn't spying exactly. She had been lingering in the dining hall over a cup of cocoa, looking over some shots she had taken on the *Clarion,* Camby Hall's student newspaper, of which she was the star photographer, when P.A. walked in with Alison. It wasn't unusual for P.A. to pop up unexpectedly in the main building, or one of the classrooms, but she always steered clear of the dining hall. *Smart lady!* Faith thought. After all, she had a beautiful residence on campus — the old Canby home — and a live-in cook.

"Good morning, Ms. Allardyce," the girls behind the counter chirped. They were smiling from ear to ear as if Princess Diana had just dropped in.

Ha! They barely grunted to us! Faith thought

disgustedly. She grinned, watching them scurry around trying to find a decent cup of coffee for P.A. *Lots of luck,* she thought grimly. When she saw them headed for a table near the window, she quickly slid into the seat that Shelley had left. She was partially hidden by the fern, and she strained to hear their conversation.

"I would have asked Mrs. Benbow to make us breakfast," P.A. was saying to Alison, "but we're repainting the downstairs rooms, and everything is a disaster."

"Oh, this is fine," Alison murmured. "I'm glad I had a chance to talk to you."

P.A. took a sip of her coffee, and an odd expression crossed her face. Faith peered out cautiously and studied her. Even at this early hour, she was perfectly put together. She was a tall, elegant woman who favored tailored tweeds and simple jewelry. Her blonde hair was swept back in a French twist and on this chilly morning, she was wearing a gray wool suit, a white silk blouse, and tiny pearl earrings. She and Alison made an unlikely pair, Faith thought. Alison was dressed as flamboyantly as ever, in an Indian print skirt with about five silk scarves knotted around her waist. She was leaning forward, talking eagerly, and every now and then she'd tuck back a lock of auburn hair that had strayed into her eyes.

Faith would have had the perfect vantage

point to eavesdrop if one of the cooks hadn't gotten a sudden urge to clean the giant coffee urn just then. *Today of all days!* Faith thought in despair. The coffee pot probably hadn't been cleaned since World War II, but now the cook was attacking it with an electric brush that made a noise like the Concorde. It was impossible to hear what Alison was telling P.A., and after a futile attempt at lip-reading, Faith gave up. *I'll just have to wait till lunch time, like everybody else,* she decided, but she hoped that the way Alison and P.A. were smiling and laughing was a good sign.

CHAPTER THREE

When Faith dashed into the dining hall at noon, she was disappointed to find Dana, Shelley, and Casey already eating lunch — and no sign of Alison anywhere. She hurried through the salad bar line, glancing over every now and then at her three friends, who were talking excitedly. *They must have heard some good news about Florida*, she thought. She decided to forget about dessert — after all, who could get excited over banana pudding — and hurried to join them.

"Anyway," Dana was saying breathlessly, "Alison said she'll be here sometime tomorrow night — isn't that great?"

"Isn't what great?" Faith said, sliding into an empty seat. "And where's Alison? I thought we were all supposed to get together for a pow-wow on Florida." She paused, and then pretended to glower at them. "And how come you guys didn't wait for me?"

"Sorry, Faith," Shelley laughed. "We just

27

couldn't wait to dig into all this wilted lettuce and rubbery tomatoes." She poked a fork into her salad, and lowered her voice to a whisper. "Did you take a look at today's special — the Mystery Meat? I couldn't believe it. The girl ahead of me ordered it. If you scrape away all that wallpaper-paste sauce, it's actually *gray* underneath — "

"And it has blubber on it," Dana piped up. "The cook really outdid herself this time. I think she fried Moby Dick."

"Please, not while I'm eating," Casey muttered.

"Will somebody please fill me in about Florida?" Faith pleaded. "Or are you going to keep me in suspense while you make whale jokes?"

Dana, Shelley, and Casey exchanged looks. "Okay, I'll tell her," Shelley said. She loved an audience, and couldn't resist giving a long, theatrical sigh. "Well, the fact is, Faith . . ." she paused, drawing out the moment for all it was worth . . . "that Alison couldn't meet us today because something important came up. We're getting a transfer student at Canby Hall and she's going to be here tomorrow night." She smiled expectantly.

"Are you putting me on?" Faith said impatiently. "That's the big news?"

"There's more," Shelley said. "You're not going to believe this, but she's from Paris!" Her blue eyes were brimming with excitement. Shelley had never met anyone from Europe, but she knew that she was going to be great friends with this new transfer student. After all, she'd been an outsider herself — a country girl in the midst of sophisticated city girls — so she knew exactly how the new girl would feel. And if Iowa was a long way from Canby Hall, well, just think what it would be like for somebody from Paris. . . . Shelley shook her head sympathetically. She was determined to do everything she could to make the French girl feel right at home at Canby Hall.

"She's from Paris? Wow," Faith muttered.

"And that's not all," Shelley added in a hushed tone. "She's supposed to be a countess." When Faith looked at her incredulously, she said to Dana, "Isn't that right? That's what you said — a countess."

Dana sipped her coffee thoughtfully. "Well, we're not completely sure about that," she hedged. "But we do know that her name is Nicole Brisbet, and the four of us are sort of officially in charge of her." She paused and glanced around the table. "P.A. told Alison that she definitely wants Nicole to live in Baker House, so we can watch out for her, and make her feel welcome. You know, make her part of the gang."

"Who's she rooming with?" Faith asked. "The doubles and triples are all full, aren't they?"

"That's right. She'll have to get a single. Alison is going to put her in that corner room at the end of the hall. It's not the best room in the world, but it'll be okay when they fix it up. Alison and P.A. are in Greenleaf right now doing some shopping. They're picking out new drapes and a bedspread for her."

At this, Faith burst out laughing, and three pairs of startled eyes turned to her.

"What's the joke?" Dana demanded.

Faith grinned. "I just had a sudden picture of P.A. and Alison going shopping together. Can't you just see it? They like completely different things. P.A. will pick out something navy blue and starchy, very practical —"

"And Alison will pick out a wild print in orange burlap!" Casey volunteered. "You're right. Poor Nicole. She's going to have the weirdest room in Baker House."

"Exactly," Faith agreed. "Well, when did all this happen?" she continued when the laughter died down. "I saw P.A. and Alison at breakfast together this morning, and I thought they were talking about the Florida trip."

"They were talking about Nicole," Dana said with a smile. "And Alison said to tell you you'll never make it in the C.I.A., Faith. She spotted you behind that potted plant right away."

"Okay, so I'm not Mata Hari," Faith groaned. "Hey, I just thought of something.

Does anybody know if Nicole speaks English? If she doesn't, we're in for a big problem."

"I'm sure she does," Dana said. "They study it in school over there."

"I sure hope her English is better than my French," Shelley said wistfully.

"If it isn't, she'll starve to death," Faith said cheerfully. "She won't be able to order anything at Pizza Pete's. We better teach her three words right away — pepperoni, double cheese, and take-out."

"That's more than three words," Casey objected.

"So who's counting?" Faith countered. She pushed away her salad dish and glanced at her watch. "Hey gang, we don't have much time left. What's the story on Florida — does anybody know if it's off or on?"

"I'm sure it's still on," Dana said. "Alison was in a mad rush, and she wanted to tell me about Nicole. We can catch her later and get the verdict." She draped a lock of long brown hair over one eye and said teasingly, "I'm already planning on a dynamite new wardrobe, so it better be still on."

"But all our summer clothes are at home," Faith pointed out. "We don't have anything to pack."

"That's the best part," Dana said. "Don't you get it? We've got the perfect excuse to buy new clothes when we get there." She sighed happily. "I hear they've got miles and miles of fantastic shops along the beach. T-shirts, bikinis, and sun suits. . . ."

Faith said something in reply, but Shelley was only half-listening. All the talk about clothes made her depressed. She just had to do something about her figure before they left for Florida! She wasn't plump exactly, but she wasn't stylishly thin, either, she decided. The truth was, she only weighed a few pounds more than her roommates, but somehow it was distributed differently.

She sneaked a look at her friends. Dana could have stepped right off the pages of a fashion magazine, with her long, slender arms and legs. Shelley didn't know how she did it, but she managed to be thin and curvy at the same time, just like Cheryl Tiegs. Everybody kidded her that she could wear a bag and make it look like a million dollars. In fact, last Halloween, she had done just that — she had worn a burlap bag as a minidress — and had looked sensational.

On this particular day, Dana was wearing a bright yellow turtleneck and black wool pants. Nothing special, maybe, but the pants fit perfectly, with a knife-sharp crease, and Dana had twisted a black and yellow scarf around her waist for a belt. It was little touches like the scarf and the tiny silver rings on her fingers that added up to a unique "Dana" look. No one else had it, or could even attempt it.

And Casey and Faith were another story. They dressed more casually than Dana, in jeans and sweaters, but they had that long, lean look that Shelley admired. And they were thin. Definitely thin, Shelley thought enviously. They had such tiny little waists, they had to keep tucking their sweaters back in their jeans. Shelley's sweaters *never* came out of her jeans. She was built exactly like her mother, she realized. She looked . . . what was the word her father always used to describe her? Solid! That was it. Solid. How awful. . . .

"Earth to Shelley," Faith said, breaking into her thoughts. Shelley looked up to see that everyone was struggling into their winter coats, obviously waiting for her. "Are you really that crazy over hot chocolate? You've been stirring that cup for ages."

"While we're standing here waiting for you," Dana said, giving her a funny look. "We've got exactly five minutes to get to our fifth period classes."

"I don't have anything till seventh period," Shelley said quickly. "Why don't you just go on without me?"

"You're going to sit here till seventh period?" Casey said in amazement.

"No, of course not," Shelley laughed. "I've got some errands to do." She whipped out a notebook and pretended to be writing furiously. "I've got loads of things to do before we go to Florida," she explained. "I think I'd better make a list before I tackle them."

Faith looked unconvinced, but Shelley smiled warmly at her. *If only they'd hurry up and go*, she thought irritably. She'd thought of a plan — a terrific plan — but she didn't dare tell anyone about it. And she certainly couldn't put it in action until her friends had left. She managed to give an enormous yawn. "I think I'll just get a refill on the hot chocolate, and get up the energy to get going. You go on ahead. Honestly." *Just leave!* she pleaded silently.

"Are you sure you're okay?" Dana asked.

Shelley nodded. "Sure I am." She pointed to the clock above the serving line. "And you're going to be late for fifth period."

"Oops, so we are," Dana said hurriedly. "Okay, Shel, we'll catch you later."

Shelley smiled as they disappeared in a flurry of camel coats and hats and mufflers. The moment they were out of sight, she dashed to the bank of phones against the wall. The Greenleaf directory was small, and she found what she was looking for immediately. She hesitated, took a deep breath, and then dialed a number. She suddenly felt nervous, even a little silly, and the receiver felt slippery in her hand. The woman who answered the phone was so nice, though, and so reassuring, that all her doubts were dispelled. And best of all, they'd be glad to see her that afternoon. Right away, in fact! Shelley breathed a sigh of relief and hung up the phone.

She felt excited, adventurous. And just a little nervous. Was she making a mistake? Of course not! She was doing exactly the right thing. She wouldn't tell anybody about it, though, she decided. At least, not at first. Let them wait and see the results, that was by far the best way.

She giggled. Wait till they saw the new Shelley!

"Was Shelley acting a little strange, or do I have an overactive imagination?" Dana was asking Faith that very minute. They were hurrying to their classes in the main building, and had their heads bent down to avoid the howling wind that was ripping across the campus.

"Yes, you have an overactive imagination, and as for Shelley. . . ." She paused, thinking. "I don't know. She didn't seem like herself, but you know, sometimes she gets quiet like that."

Dana nodded. "I think Shelley likes to keep things to herself sometimes. I'm sure she'll snap back to reality when we see Alison this afternoon. I can hardly wait to see what she and P.A. picked out in Greenleaf."

"Maybe it's not as bad as you think," Faith

offered. "You know, We could always con-
tribute some posters to liven things up." She
grinned as they parted in the main hallway.
"Here's my stop," she said, heading toward
algebra. "Catch you later, Dana."

Dana smiled absently and continued on to
Spanish class. What *was* wrong with Shelley,
she wondered. She had been in an absolute
daze at lunch, and all that talk about making
lists! What in the world was she talking
about?

Someone jostled her elbow just as she was
zipping in the door to Spanish class. "Oh,
sorry," Pamela said in a bored voice. "Every
time I have to come to this class, I put my
mind on automatic pilot. It makes it less pain-
ful that way." She gave an elaborate sigh.

"Spanish isn't so bad," Dana said defensively. Usually she didn't even bother talking
to Pamela, but for some reason, the girl's
sarcastic one-liners seemed more annoying
than usual.

"I don't know what it's good for," Pamela
said breezily. "Although I suppose it's okay if
you want to go shopping in Acapulco. But the
last time Yvonne and I were there, everyone
spoke English anyway. Everyone who was
anyone, if you know what I mean," she added.

Dana sighed. "I know what you mean," she
said curtly. Pamela was a hopeless snob. Suddenly Dana had an idea. She was sure that
Pamela hadn't heard about Nicole, and it

would be fun to shake her up a little.

She glanced towards the door. Luckily, Mr. Ramirez, the Spanish teacher, was lost in conversation with a student, and with any luck, class would start late. "I suppose you've heard about Nicole Brisbet coming here," Dana began lazily.

Pamela looked up with interest. "Nicole Brisbet? Who is she?"

Dana forced a look of surprise. "You mean you haven't heard? *The* Nicole Brisbet — the French countess — is moving into Baker House tomorrow!"

"Oh, *that* Nicole Brisbet," Pamela said slowly. "Yes, I think I did hear something about that." She was desperately trying to cover up her surprise. "She's from . . . uh. . . ."

"She's from Paris, of course," Dana said smugly. "You surely didn't think she was from the provinces, did you? I mean, she's not exactly what you'd call a farm girl, is she?" She managed a light, wordly laugh, the kind that Pamela always gave.

"No, she certainly isn't," Pamela agreed quickly.

"It's quite an honor for the school, you know," Dana went on. "After all, with a background like hers . . . well, she could go anywhere she wanted."

"Oh, of course," Pamela said. "I think I did hear something about her coming here, now that you mention it," she went on, lowering her voice. "Although it's not common knowledge, is it?"

"No, just a . . . select few . . . know about it," Dana told her, trying not to giggle. She couldn't believe how impressed Pamela was! She was leaning forward, hanging on Dana's every word. Dana knew she was just dying for class to be over so she could go spread the news about Nicole. And of course, knowing Pamela, she'd make it look as if she was personally responsible for Nicole coming to Canby Hall!

"So she's from Paris," Pamela said, twirling the end of a silken string of blonde hair around her finger. "I wonder if she knows Paul and Marie Gemel? I spent an absolutely fantastic summer with them a couple of years ago. The Gemels have this wonderful little apartment right off the Champs-Elysees. Of course, it's not so little," she added with a laugh. "Fourteen rooms, and those gorgeous French doors that have glass from the floor to the ceiling." She sighed, and inspected her magenta fingernails.

"Well, you'll just have to ask her, won't you?" Dana said sweetly.

"Oh, I will," Pamela said earnestly. "We probably have loads of friends in common. In fact, who knows? Maybe I've already run into Nicole at something. Although Yvonne and I always spend most of our time on the Riviera. We try to avoid Paris because it's gotten so crowded lately. All those dreadful tourists. Still, j'adore Paris," she purred. "And I detest Spanish!" she said coldly, as Mr. Ramirez rapped on the desk to start the class.

A few minutes later, as they were lost in the history of Grenada, Pamela sneaked a puzzled look at Dana over the top of her Spanish book. She was still trying to figure out who Nicole Brisbet was. And why Dana seemed to know so much about her, when Pamela herself didn't! After all, she reasoned, Dana was a nobody. *If anybody should know about Nicole Brisbet, it should be me.*

She frowned and bit her lip, just as Dana looked over and grinned at her. It was nice to know that she'd managed to ruin Pamela's afternoon.

CHAPTER FOUR

"What do you mean you can't see me this afternoon? We had a date," Tom was saying plaintively a few hours later.

Shelley cradled the phone against her neck, so she could sneak a quick look at her watch. She's have to get off the phone fast, or she'd be late for her appointment at Heavenly Bodies, "Uh, Tom, it's kind of complicated. I'm calling from a pay phone in Greenleaf —"

"Good. Stay right where you are," he said quickly, "and we'll split a double pepperoni and sausage at Pizza Pete's."

Shelley smiled. In another minute, she knew she'd weaken, cancel the appointment, and keep the date with Tom. He was so adorable! He wasn't the only boy in her life. There was also Paul, her boyfriend back home in Iowa, but Tom was very special to her.

"I've got things to do," she protested.

"More important than seeing me?" he said teasingly. His voice was warm and deep, and if Shelley hadn't been in immediate danger of frostbite, she would have stayed on the phone forever.

"Not more important," she sighed. "But . . . necessary." If she told Tom what she was really up to, she knew he'd burst out laughing. He'd think she was out of her mind. Boys just had no idea what girls really went through to stay thin and attractive.

"Well, what about tonight? I'll meet you in the lounge after dinner."

"No, honestly, I can't." Shelley ran a hand nervously through her short, curly blonde hair. "I've got a million things I've got to do, and besides that, we've got a new girl arriving tonight."

"A likely story," Tom kidded her.

"I'm serious," Shelley insisted. "We've got a French student moving into Baker House tonight, and — and we're having a welcoming party for her," she said, in a burst of inspiration. She stomped her feet. The door was off the phone booth, and the wind whipped mercilessly around her bare legs. She wished for the dozenth time that she hadn't decided to change out of her jeans and leg-warmers into a skirt and blouse.

Tom gave a long sigh. "I guess I'll have to be lonely," he said finally. "Just me and my math book. . . ."

Shelley giggled. "We're going to see each other tomorrow night, you know. We're supposed to be tripling with Dana and Faith."

"I know that," he said in an aggrieved tone. "But that's . . . " he paused, figuring rapidly ". . . twenty-eight hours away. An eternity!"

"Hardly an eternity," Shelley said drily. Sometimes Tom was so melodramatic. But of course, that's what had attracted her to him in the first place. They both shared a love of the stage, and they'd actually met at an audition for a Canby Hall-Oakley Prep production. "Listen, Tom, I really have to run. I'll see you tomorrow, okay?"

"I'll try to survive till then. And remember, you owe me one."

"One what?" Shelley said innocently.

"A kiss, of course."

"Just one?" Shelley laughed and hung up. She pulled up the collar on her good wool coat, and hurried along Oak Street. The January sky was a flat gray, like the kind she used to see in Iowa, and she was sure it would snow before the night was over. Poor Nicole! she thought. She wondered if it was even safe to fly in weather like this. Nicole was supposed to catch a connecting flight from New York to Boston, and Alison was going to pick her up at the airport.

A few minutes later, she forgot about Nicole, because she found the address she wanted. Heavenly Bodies, the sign proclaimed in giant pink letters. *Well, that's what I want, a heavenly body,* she thought, pushing open a rose-colored door. *But it's going to take a miracle to get one!* she added, smiling at her own joke.

Everything was pink and white inside Heavenly Bodies, everything from the plush ivory carpet to the bubble-gum wallpaper, to the peach-and-white-striped chairs. Even Cindy, her personal figure consultant, was pink and white. Cindy was a bubbly redhead with creamy skin, and had the most amazing figure Shelley had ever seen. And she was dressed — naturally — in a shocking pink leotard.

"So you just want to tone up a little in case you suddenly go to Florida," Cindy was saying.

Shelley tried not to stare at Cindy's remarkable shape, and said tentatively, "I suppose it sounds silly. . . ."

"No, it doesn't sound silly at all," Cindy said cheerfully, whipping out a tape measure. "You know what they say," she went on, "getting into a bikini is the moment of truth!"

Ugh! Shelley thought.

Finally, Cindy stopped measuring and writing on a chart and sat down next to Shelley. "Well, Shelley, take a look at this. I've done your personal figure analysis chart —"

"How bad is it?" Shelley blurted out.

"Not bad at all," Cindy laughed. "But, as you can see, you've got a few trouble spots, mostly the hips and thighs. It's nothing the machines can't handle, though." She stood up and tapped Shelley lightly on the shoulder. "Let's get started, shall we? I'll show you around the gym and you can start on your workout today. Everything you need to know is right on this chart —"

"Today?" Shelley interrupted. "I hadn't really planned . . . I mean, I need to get back to the dorm for dinner."

Cindy's pink and white smile faded, and her mouth tightened in a frown. "Believe me, Shelley, if you want to lose these inches before you go to Florida, you don't have a minute to waste." She looked at her clipboard and shrugged. "Of course, it's your body," she said. "And if you're not really interested in improving it —"

"But I am!" Shelley said quickly. "Show me what I have to do," she added grimly. What did it matter if she missed dinner! She'd think of an excuse to tell her friends. . . .

"Where in the world is Shel?" Dana yelled to Faith over the noise of the blow-dryer that evening. "She's going to make us late!" It was seven-twenty-five, and Alison had asked the three roommates and Casey to come up to The Penthouse at seven-thirty sharp to meet Nicole.

"I can't imagine what happened to her," Faith said. Her thick black hair was still damp from the shower, and she ran her fingers through it. She liked to wear her hair that way, soft and natural, framing her face in a tangle of curls. She grabbed a white turtleneck sweater out of the drawer, and wriggled into her best jeans. "Do you think we should say something to Alison?" she said hesitantly. "You don't think something awful's happened to her, do you?"

Dana shook her head. "I was surprised when she missed dinner," she said thoughtfully, "but now that I think of it, she did mention something about seeing Tom this afternoon. Let's wait awhile, and see what happens. Maybe they had dinner in Greenleaf, and lost track of the time."

"Maybe," Faith said doubtfully. "Speaking of time. . . ."

"I know — we're late!" Dana turned off the dryer and added a touch of lip gloss.

"I'm glad we're getting a chance to meet Nicole ahead of everybody else," Faith said a minute later, as they climbed the stairs to Alison's apartment.

"Me, too." Dana smiled. "Alison said that Nicole would feel overwhelmed if she had to meet everybody in Baker House at once. Plus, she's going to have jet lag and be really wiped out tonight."

"I wonder what she's like?" Faith said softly, as Dana rapped on Alison's door. "If she's Parisian, she's probably really wealthy and sophisticated —" A sudden, awful thought crossed her mind. "You don't think she's like

Pamela, do you?" she whispered. "Because I
don't think I could *take* another Pamela."

"I think you're safe," Dana answered.
"There couldn't be two Pamelas in the
world!"

Alison opened the door wide with a bright
smile. "Hi, gang. C'mon in and meet a new
friend. Casey's already here, and hey . . .
where's Shelley?"

"She's, uh . . ." Faith began.

"She'll be here in a few minutes," Dana
said smoothly.

"Oh, okay," Alison said, looking a little
puzzled. Dana noticed that Alison had dressed
up for the occasion, in her best Indian gauzy
blouse, and a soft brown and yellow skirt she
had bought in Peru. She led them into the
living room, and the two girls had their first
glimpse of Nicole. "Faith Thompson and
Dana Morrison, this is Nicole Brisbet," Alison said.

For a moment, there was dead silence. Faith
and Dana exchanged a look, and Dana was immediately aware of three things.

Nicole Brisbet was nothing in the world
like Pamela Young.

Nicole, with her white ankle socks, Mary
Jane shoes, and Alice-in-Wonderland headband, was wearing what any normal teenage
girl would be wearing — if the year were
1952!

Nicole Brisbet looked about twelve years old.

Dana recovered first. "Hi, Nicole. I'm glad you're staying in Baker House with us." She stopped and clapped her hand over her mouth. "Ohmigosh!," she said, flushing, "do you speak English?"

Nicole came to life then, too, and laughed. "Probably as well as you do," she said teasingly. "I've been studying it for nine years." She stood up, then, and walked over to them. "I'm very glad to meet you both." She shook hands solemnly with each of them, and for a moment everyone stood there awkwardly, wondering what to do next.

Alison broke the silence. "Well, let's sit down and relax, everybody. There's plenty of food, so help yourself, Nicole." She gestured to the coffee table that was piled high with snacks. Besides the usual assortment of potato chips and dip, there were tiny cheese sandwiches and a chafing dish fiilled with meatballs in a rich tomato sauce. "I wasn't sure what you liked, so I put out a little of everything," Alison explained. She smiled. "I figured you probably didn't eat on the plane."

Nicole laughed. "Not didn't. Couldn't! The food on the plane was like . . . false food." No one said anything, and she looked at them expectantly. "Is that how you say it?" she said hesitantly. "False food?"

Dana looked at her blankly, but Faith giggled. "Fake food. That's what you mean, Nicole."

"Yes, that's it exactly," Nicole said happily when everyone laughed. "It was like fake food. It came in a little cardboard house — and you ate it with tiny knives and forks. Like a doll would use." She shrugged. "It was bizarre." She gave the word a very French twist, so it came out "bee-zar."

"Well, please don't judge all American food by what you get on the airlines," Alison said. She opened some cans of soda and started passing out plates and napkins.

"And don't judge it by the food here at Canby Hall, either," Dana muttered. "Have you taken Nicole to the dining hall yet?" she asked Alison.

"No, I thought I'd leave that up to you tomorrow," Alison replied. "Reality is too hard to face after an eighteen-hour trip, right, Nicole?"

"Right," Nicole agreed. She speared a meatball with a toothpick and popped it in her mouth. "Bon!" she said enthusiastically. "Very good."

The conversation turned to school, then, and Nicole asked Alison a barrage of questions about Canby Hall. How many girls there were, what they were like, if the school was very strict, if the classes were hard. . . .

Dana let her mind wander, studying Nicole.

There was something strange about her, she decided. Maybe the French girl felt Dana's eyes on her, because she self-consciously tucked her ruffled dress around her knees, and hugged her arms to her chest. Why in the world was she dressed like that! Dana wondered. Her blue-and-white flowered dress looked like something a four-year-old would wear to a birthday party. And the pink cardigan sweater — buttoned to the *neck*, yet! — certainly didn't help. If ever there was someone in need of a make-over, it was Nicole.

Dana glanced over at Faith, who shrugged slightly. Nicole was going to have a really tough time at Canby Hall, Dana decided, and it was a good thing she was going to have the girls in 407, plus Casey, as her friends. She was going to need all the help she could get. The other girls were going to think she was odd — to say the least — and as for boys . . . Dana sighed. She had planned on asking her boyfriend, Randy Crowell, if he could get a date for Nicole for Friday night, but it was obviously hopeless. Who'd want to go out with a twelve-year-old?

Faith couldn't keep her eyes off Nicole, and was thinking exactly the same thing as Dana. Nicole was just the opposite of what she had expected. She wasn't the high-fashion, sophisticated type at all. In fact, she looked like a baby! Why was she wearing that awful get-up? Faith wondered. She squinted her eyes, and tried to imagine what Nicole would look like if she were dressed like a normal high school kid. Her figure wasn't bad, she thought, at least what you could see of it under that kitchen-curtain dress.

And her face was pretty — or at least, it could be. She looked pale, practically white as a sheet, but that was probably because she was exhausted from the trip. And she wasn't wearing any makeup, Not even lipstick, or a touch of mascara. Her brown eyes were set far apart, and would look terrific with just a little shadow, Faith thought. Faith had developed quite an eye for color and contrast from her work in photography, and she looked at Nicole objectively, thinking about what she would do if she had the chance.

Nicole really did have possibilities. Her features looked ordinary at first glance, but her eyes were a beautiful almond shape and she had a bright smile, with perfect white teeth. The hair was all wrong, though. Nobody wore her hair trailing down her back in a long braid these days. And just in case any stray locks were tempted to peek out, Nicole was wearing that awful headband that yanked her hair straight back from her forehead. It was almost as if she *wanted* to make herself unattractive. Very strange . . . Faith decided.

Faith forced her attention back to the conversation, just as Alison was saying, "Don't expect to accomplish too much in the first week or two, Nicole. After all, it's going to take time to adjust to a new country, and a new way of life. . . ."

"But schools everywhere are the same, are they not?" Nicole asked reasonably. "Everywhere there is the *devoir* . . . the homework," she corrected herself rapidly. "After all, that is the reason we go to school — to learn, to study, to improve ourselves." She folded her hands on her lap, as if she were reciting a lesson.

Alison looked a little surprised. "Well, yes, of course," she admitted. "Academic work is very important here at Canby Hall, but other things are important, too." She glanced at Faith, Dana, and Casey. "Friendships, and learning about people, about different ways of looking at things . . . that's part of education, too." She smiled hopefully at Nicole. "We want you to have fun at Canby Hall, you know."

"You go to school to have fun?" Nicole said softly. "Ah, you have a strange country with strange ideas." She smiled, shook her head sadly, and took another meatball.

Alison's eyes met Dana's for an instant. *Nicole is going to take some getting used to,* her expression said.

CHAPTER FIVE

W^{here were you?"} Dana demanded when she and Faith got back to 407. Shelley was sprawled on her bed, looking paler than Nicole, and she barely raised her head to look at them. "Honestly, Shelley, even Alison asked about you. How could you forget we were supposed to meet Nicole tonight!" She was half-annoyed and half-relieved to see that Shelley was safely back in the dorm.

"I was in Greenleaf and I lost track of time," Shelley said weakly. She was still dressed in her blouse and skirt, and she swung her long legs over the side of the bed. Every muscle ached and she wondered how she'd ever make it into her pajamas without Dana and Faith noticing that she was in pain.

"What's wrong?" Faith asked, watching her.

"Wrong?" Shelley said innocently. "Nothing's wrong. I'm just a little tired." She faked a yawn and tried a tentative stretch. It hurt too much, though, and she quickly dropped her hands back to her sides.

Faith laughed. "You remind me of my aunt's cat, Simba."

"Well, I suppose that's a compliment," Shelley said between gritted teeth. "My acting teacher said that cats are the most graceful creatures on earth." She wriggled painfully out of bed and managed to make it over to the dresser by taking very little steps.

Dana burst out laughing. "You better tell her about Simba, Faith."

"He's seventeen years old and he's got arthritis," Faith explained. "And you're walking just like him. Honestly, Shelley, what in the world is wrong with you?"

"I told you — nothing!" Shelley snapped. She grabbed her towel. "And now, if you'll excuse me, I'm going to take a shower." She walked out of the room with as much dignity as she could muster, although it was tough to look dignified since she was practically hobbling. Cindy had warned her that she might be a little sore after her first workout, but this was ridiculous! She felt like she might never walk again.

She took a long hot shower, and was on the way back to 407 when she noticed that the door at the end of the hall was open very slightly. Of course — Nicole. There was a light on, and the soft sound of guitar music filtered down the hall. Shelley hesitated.

There would be plenty of time to meet Nicole tomorrow, and yet she felt a little guilty about not going to the welcoming party. Maybe it would be better to make her apologies now and get it over with.

She tapped softly on the door and a young girl with long brown hair opened it almost immediately. "Yes?" she said timidly.

She looks like a kid! Shelley thought. She quickly recovered and smiled. "You're Nicole, right? I'm Shelley Hyde."

The girl seemed friendlier then, and swung the door open wide. "You're Dana and Faith's roommate, no?"

"No," Shelley agreed. "I mean, yes. I'm their roommate. And I'm really sorry I missed you earlier at Alison's."

"That's okay." Nicole sat on the bed and stared at her. "Sit down, if you can find a spot. I'll have to straighten all this out tomorrow. I just couldn't face unpacking tonight." There were piles of clothes tumbling out of open suitcases, and a box full of heavy sweaters had spilled out on the floor. Shelley noticed a pair of skis propped up against one wall.

The room was a mess, but it had possibilities, Shelley decided. She smiled when she saw the bedspread. Navy blue, tailored, with white trim. Classic P.A. But someone — probably Alison — had added a bright red throw rug, a director's chair with a red canvas back, and a set of navy and white pin-stripe drapes. All it needed was some posters and a few throw pillows. She'd have to ask for some contributions tomorrow. Maybe Dana could part with one of her Joffrey Ballet posters, and she had a giant blow-up of Rick Springfield she could donate. . . .

Nicole interrupted her thoughts. "I hope my radio did not disturb anyone," she said apologetically. " I wasn't sure about the rules here."

"Oh, no," Shelley said quickly. "I stopped by because I saw the light on under your door."

"I didn't know if there was such a thing as . . . lights out." She laughed and shrugged. "I asked, but Alison was pretty vague about things like that."

"She never worries about the small stuff," Shelley agreed. "When you get to know her, you'll find she's tough about some things, and pretty relaxed about others. She's really fair, though, and everybody in Baker House is crazy over her."

"I can see that."

There was a long silence, then, and Shelley stood up uncertainly. "Well, I know you want to get to bed. I just stopped by to say hello."

Nicole pulled her powder blue robe more tightly around her and stood up too. "I'm glad you did, Shelley. I hope we can be friends." She walked Shelley to the door.

"Definitely. We're already neighbors, so remember, if you want anything, just come down to 407."

As she made her way down the hall, Shelley shook her head over her encounter with Nicole. She was a strange girl, she decided, both timid and self-assured. She looked really young, but maybe that was because she wasn't wearing any makeup, and she had that long hair trailing down her back.

Something didn't quite fit, though, and she struggled to remember what it was. An image jumped into her mind, and suddenly she knew. It was the eyes. Nicole's eyes didn't look young at all. They were deep brown, fringed with black lashes, and they looked . . . knowing. Shelley shrugged. It was going to be hard to figure out Nicole.

When Dana stopped by Nicole's room to take her to breakfast the next morning, her heart sank. Nicole was wearing another one of those ruffly pinafore dresses, and the same patent leather shoes. She probably has an endless supply of them, Dana thought despairingly. She debated whether or not she should say something and decided against it. Maybe once Nicole saw how the other girls were dressed, she'd do something about her own wardrobe. Nicole's dark eyes flickered over Dana's designer jeans and creamy yellow sweater, but she never said a word.

"Casey, Faith, and Shelley are downstairs in the lounge," Dana said cheerfully. "We thought it would be fun if we all went over to the dining hall together."

"That's nice," Nicole said simply.

She didn't seem to have much to say as they crossed the campus, but Dana chalked it up to the fact that she was probably still tired from the long trip. Luckily, Casey could talk enough for half a dozen people, and she gave Nicole a running commentary on the history of Canby Hall, plus a complete rundown on the teachers and courses. Nicole listened politely, but didn't seem too impressed.

She's probably homesick already, Shelley thought sympathetically. She resolved to spend as much time with her as she could during the next few weeks. She edged over close to Nicole when they got to the dining hall, and handed her a tray. "You get the silverware here, Nicole. And you can go through the line as many times as you want."

Nicole took one look at the steaming counter with its pancakes and scrambled eggs and gave a delicate shudder. "No, no thank you," she said faintly. "I never eat breakfast."

"What do you mean?" Shelley said, astonished. "Aren't you hungry?" Shelley couldn't figure her out. Surely even French people knew that breakfast was the most important meal of the day!

"Just coffee, that's all I ever have." She spotted the giant coffee urn further down the line and bypassed Shelley and her friends. "It is permitted to go ahead? Coffee is all I want."

"Sure, go ahead," Shelley said, a little hurt. "We'll catch up with you."

Nicole took a cup of coffee with extra cream, and headed for a long table by the window. One whole wall of the dining hall was glass, and it faced onto a meadow that was covered with a thick blanket of snow. At that precise moment, Pamela Young was heading for the same table. She, too, was holding a cup of coffee, and was engrossed in a newspaper. She nearly collided with Nicole, as they both reached for the same chair.

"Sorry," Pamela said automatically. Then she did a double take. "Aren't you Nicole? The transfer from Paris?"

"Yes," Nicole said, a little wearily.

"I'm Pamela Young. My mother's movies are very popular in your country."

"Ah. . . ." Nicole's face took on a new, interested expression. "Your mother is an actress?"

"She's Yvonne Young," Pamela said smugly, pulling out a chair. "Her last movie was called *Summer Splendor*, and some of it was filmed on the Riviera."

"Yes, exactly," Nicole said excitedly. "At Juan-les-Pins." She beamed at Pamela. "I was spending the day there with some friends and we watched the filming. Your mother is very beautiful. You look a lot like her, you know."

"Thanks." Pamela gave a self-satisfied smile, just as Dana and Faith sat down. "I simply love Juan-les-Pins. Do you spend much time there?"

Nicole nodded. "My family keeps a yacht in Cannes, so we spend a lot of our time on the coast . . . Nice, Antibes, St. Tropez."

Pamela gave a theatrical sigh. "Oh, you don't know how good it feels to hear those names again. They're magical places to me. I adore the Riviera. It's so French, and so . . . expensive." She leaned forward and said confidentially, "I hate to say it, Nicole, but you're going to find that Canby Hall is very . . . how shall I say it . . . provincial."

"Vraiment?" Nicole said, lapsing into French.

"Absolument," Pamela answered.

Shelley heard the last part of this exchange, and said happily to Casey, "Oh, isn't that nice. Nicole found someone to speak French with." She and Casey sat down across from Nicole, and she added, "I still can't believe you're not having breakfast."

"A smart move," Pamela said approvingly. "The food here will kill you," she said flatly. "In fact, I've got a fantastic idea. I'd love to treat you to dinner tonight. There's a French restaurant in Greenleaf called the Auberge. It won't be up to your standards, of course, but they do a pretty good job with steak and veal. Would you like to give it a try?"

Nicole hesitated and looked at Dana. "Well, I'd like to, but I'm supposed to stick close to Dana and her friends. All of us were planning on eating here in the dining hall tonight."

"Really, Nicole," Dana said, "we're not your keepers. If you'd like to have dinner with Pamela, you should go ahead."

"Well, in that case," Nicole said calmly, "I accept. Thank you very much." There was an awkward silence, and then Nicole looked thoughtfully at Pamela. "How did you happen to come to Canby Hall? I would have thought you would prefer to live with your mother."

"Well, I would," Pamela said, flushing a little. It was the first time that Dana had ever seen her look uncomfortable. "But her schedule is so crazy. . . ." She waved her hands in a helpless gesture. "She never knows where she'll be from week to week."

"Yes, I can understand that. My parents live exactly the same way. The Film Festival in Cannes, the Grand Prix in Monaco, Oktoberfest in Munich. . . . They travel almost constantly." She sipped her coffee, and made a face. "Not quite *cafe au lait,* is it?" she said to Pamela.

"Not by a long shot!" Pamela answered with a grin. It was obvious that she enjoyed being singled out for Nicole's attention.

"We learned about *cafe au lait* in French class," Shelley said very seriously. "Don't you fill the cup half with coffee and the rest with hot —"

"Where do you live in Paris?" Pamela said, ignoring her.

Nicole delicately blotted her lips before replying. "Oh, we have an apartment just off the Champs-Elysees," she said vaguely. "And of course, we keep a place in the country near Mont St. Michel." She paused. "We also have a chalet at Chamonix for skiing. We go there nearly every weekend in the winter."

"How nice," Pamela said weakly. "An apartment, a country house, a chalet, and a yacht."

For once, Pamela is at a loss for words, Faith thought happily. It was obvious that she was impressed by Nicole — she had never paid so much attention to anyone at Canby Hall before. *I suppose Nicole is the only person here she considers an equal,* she decided. *She thinks of the rest of us as peasants.*

"If you'd like to drop by my room after school, Nicole," Pamela was saying, "I'll make you some espresso. Actually, you're not supposed to cook anything in the dorm, but I've got this marvelous little machine I picked up the last time I was in New York."

"That sounds very nice," Nicole said politely. "And if you'd like to stop by my room, I've got some French music you might like to hear — it's mostly rock and jazz, with a little reggae."

"I'd love to," Pamela squealed. "No one else here even knows what reggae is," she added, shooting a look at Shelley. "I can't believe I've finally found a kindred spirit in this place."

Dana sat silently, taking it all in. *I wonder if Nicole knows what she's found,* she thought. *And I wonder if I should warn her about Pamela. . . .*

Later that night, Dana was holding hands with her boyfriend, Randy Crowell, in the Rialto Theater. The main feature hadn't started yet, and Faith and Shelley were in the lobby with their dates, stocking up on popcorn and soft drinks. She wondered briefly what Nicole was doing — probably listening to records with Pamela, she supposed. Or maybe they were still at the Auberge having a fancy dinner. Dana felt a little guilty at deserting her on her second night at Canby Hall, but Casey had said that she'd check on her, and of course Alison would be there, too.

"Are you sure you don't want anything?" Dana asked Randy. "I can get you something while the cartoon is on." She knew that Randy was a cartoon freak, and that he wouldn't want to miss a minute of the Bugs Bunny classic that was playing.

"No, I've got everything I need right here,"

Randy said, giving her hand a little squeeze. "I think I'm going to hold on to it, too. Forever."

She smiled back at him in the darkness. She liked being with Randy. It wasn't a flash-in-the pan romance like she had had with Bret Harper last year. This was a nice, steady relationship with a boy she could count on.

Randy came from one of the big landowning families around Greenleaf, and was strictly an outdoors type. He was ruggedly handsome, with blond hair that curled around his collar, and steely gray eyes that sometimes seemed to Dana as if they could look right through her. He seemed different, more mature than the boys who went to Oakley Prep, and Dana liked that. In fact, she liked practically everything about Randy Crowell.

"So you're going to hold my hand forever," she teased him, just as Elmer Fudd flattened Bugs Bunny with a steamroller.

"Well, at least until it's time to kiss you good-night," he said thoughtfully. "And then I'll have to let go to put my arms around you." He turned to her and said in a husky voice, "Speaking of kissing. . . ."

"Yes?" she said innocently.

"There's no time like the present," he whispered, and kissed her very gently on the mouth. His lips were warm and soft, and for a moment she forgot that her friends and their dates would be joining them any second.

"You're right," she said, leaning her cheek against the rough tweed of his jacket. It was so easy to be happy and relaxed with Randy. She knew that there was something she wanted to ask him about, something that was gnawing at her mind. Oh yes, Nicole. She was going to ask him about Nicole.

"Randy," she began softly, "there's something I want to talk to you about. . . ."

"Can it wait till later?" hs whispered, bending his head close to hers.

"Well. . . ." Dana never had a chance to finish, but it didn't matter. Randy kissed her again and she made up her mind. Nicole could definitely wait until later.

CHAPTER SIX

Shelley was up early the next morning, even though it was a bitterly cold Saturday, and her bed had never seemed more inviting. She winced as her feet hit the freezing floor. Baker Hall was one of the oldest dorms on campus, and the heating system dated back to the last century. *Maybe that's why the heat never seems to make it up to the fourth floor*, she thought resignedly, as she pulled a heavy red sweater over her head.

She glanced at her watch. Seven-thirty. If she left right away, she could be at Heavenly Bodies by eight. There was no point in having breakfast, and anyway, Cindy had told her it was best to exercise on an empty stomach. She tossed her new black leotard into her purse, wriggled into jeans and tennis shoes, and let herself quietly out the door. She took a last quick look at Faith and Dana, who were curled up in quilts, dead to the world. They'd never know what she was up to, she told herself. Not until she was ready to surprise them with her new figure!

Half an hour later, she scooted into the back row of an aerobics class and tried to be as inconspicuous as possible. The teacher, who was named Cheryl, could have been Cindy's clone. She was thin, blonde, and beautiful — with the personality of a drill sergeant!

"I want to see your thighs quiver!" she shouted over the steady thump of rock music. "If you're not sweating, you're not working!" she yelled, as she made her way through the sea of gyrating bodies. Even the exercise room at Heavenly Bodies was pink and white, with red strobe lights casting dazzling patterns on the floors and ceiling. The walls were a nauseating bubble-gum pink, and Shelley felt as if she were trapped inside a giant psychedelic Kleenex box.

She struggled to keep up with the rest of the class, even though her muscles were still throbbing from the last session with the "toning" machines. Her "personalized exercise program" called for an hour of aerobics followed by an hour on the machines. Then it would be time for a weigh-in, and measuring. . . . Shelley sighed. Was it all worth it? She looked at Cheryl. Flat stomach, tiny waist, no hips. She could probably go into any store, pull a size seven bikini off the rack, and it would look sensational on her. Shelley always had trouble picking out bathing suits. Her mother used to help her, but her mother's taste ran to flowered prints and those flappy skirts that are supposed to hide your thighs, but never do.

There would be fantastic suits to choose from in Florida . . . sleek maillots cut high on the thigh, and crocheted peek-a-boo bikinis. All the suits she had seen in the fashion magazines were really daring this year, with a lot of mesh and cut-outs. Dana had already said she was going to get one of those shiny vinyl "wet look" suits the moment they got to Florida. Shelley took another look at Cheryl. Yes, it was worth it all right. She gritted her teeth and started her twenty-seventh sit-up.

"She's done her disappearing act again," Faith was saying to Dana at that precise moment. Faith had woken up, glanced at the clock, and turned over to go back to sleep, when she spotted Shelley's empty bed.

Dana pulled the quilt around her, ran a hand through her tousled brown hair and frowned. "It's strange, isn't it? Did she say anything to you about it last night?"

"Nothing," Faith replied. "Anyway, she and Tom were too involved with each other to even notice anyone else. If you remember, they insisted on walking back to Baker House alone — and they took the long way," she added meaningfully.

"I noticed," Dana said with a smile. "Randy

and I passed them in his pick-up truck and they were in a world of their own." She yawned and stretched just as they heard a light tap on the door. "A little early for visitors, isn't it?"

Faith raised her eyebrows. "Unless it's Nicole?" she whispered.

"She's probably homesick," Dana said, springing out of bed.

But it wasn't Nicole, it was Alison. "I know it's early, but I heard you guys talking," she said. "Do you mind if I get started on room check? I thought if I finish in time, I might go skating with Michael. . . ." Her voice trailed off when she noticed Shelley's empty bed. "Where's Shel? She's not in the bathroom — I just checked it."

Faith and Dana looked at each other. "We don't know," Dana said. "Unless she's got a project at the library . . ." she said uncertainly. "That must be it," she said in a firmer voice. "Shelley said she's really going to start buckling down and working hard. I know she wants to get her French grades up this quarter." She was almost positive that Shelley was nowhere near the library, but she didn't want to make Alison suspicious.

"Well, I'm glad to hear it," Alison said, sounding relieved. She was holding a cup of coffee, and she put it down carefully on the dresser. "Okay," she said in a businesslike way, "Your beds aren't made, but I won't count that, because you're in them. . . ."

"Thanks a lot," Faith teased her.

"But I need to grade the rest of the room." She opened the closet door and made a face. "I thought you girls promised to do better this week," she said to Dana.

"Closets just aren't a high-priority item with us," Faith told her.

"I'll say," Alison muttered. She ran her finger down the checklist and gave up. It would be almost impossible to give them a grade on the closet. Jeans, skirts, and dresses were jumbled together on a rod that was sagging dangerously in the middle. Blouses were hung on top of blouses, and the whole closet floor was littered with belts, hangers, and shoes.

"It's called creative disorder," Dana told her solemnly.

"It looks like the clearance rack at Macy's," Alison retorted. She made a few notes on her clipboard and shook her head. She felt like a warden every time she had to do room check, but it was a school rule. Patrice Allardyce was convinced that a neat room was the sign of an orderly mind.

"You never gave us the verdict on Florida," Dana said, hoping to divert her attention. "Is the trip off or on?" Faith had slid out of bed, and was quickly stashing her hat, muffler, and gloves under her pillow. If Alison spotted clothes on the floor, it was good for half a dozen demerits. She saw a stray sock in the corner, and hurriedly tucked that under the pillow, too.

Alison turned to Dana in surprise. "Oh, I meant to tell you about that," she said. "I've had a million things on my mind. It's yes." She went back to the clipboard.

"It's on?" Dana said, jumping out of bed. "And you've kept us in suspense all this time?"

"I just found out yesterday," Alison said calmly. "Ms. Allardyce isn't wild over the idea, but I convinced her that it would be an 'educational experience,' just like you said." She gave a wry smile. "You see, I took your advice and it paid off. I'm going to talk to Michael about it today."

"That's terrific. I can't believe she agreed to it." Dana reached past Alison to retrieve a pair of furry slippers from her closet floor.

"I think having Nicole here changed her mind," Alison said thoughtfully.

"Nicole? What does she have to do with it?"

"Well, Nicole may only be with us for a few months, just till the end of the school year, and I guess she thought it would be nice for her to see as much of the country as possible."

"I'm beginning to like Nicole already," Faith said with a grin. "If she's our ticket to Florida, then she's the best thing that ever happened to Canby Hall."

"Tell me something," Alison said, sitting

on the edge of Dana's bed. "What do you really think of Nicole?" She looked at them very seriously. "I've wanted to ask you ever since you met her."

"She seems . . . nice," Dana said cautiously. "Sort of quiet and shy, I guess. But I suppose that's because she's in a strange country."

"The reason I'm asking is . . . well, I don't want to press Nicole on you," Alison said, "but I'd like you to spend as much time with her as you could. At least in the beginning."

"That's no problem," Dana said, looking at Faith. "We can take her into Greenleaf today with us. She might get a kick out of seeing what a small New England town looks like. And we'll stop for lunch at Pizza Pete's —"

"And for ice cream at the Tutti-Frutti," Faith suggested. "We can take her to the record store and the dime store, and spend all afternoon with her."

"That sounds good," Alison said. She picked at a loose thread on Dana's bedspread and said hesitantly, "Could you do just one more favor for me?"

"For you? Anything!" Dana smiled and threw her arm around Alison's shoulder. "After all, you're the one who's taking us to Florida, right? We owe you one."

Alison smiled. "You may not be crazy over the idea, but . . . how would you feel about getting her a date for tonight?"

For a moment, there was dead silence. Faith and Dana were thinking exactly the same thing. A date for Nicole — impossible! The girls in 407 were willing to make allowances for the way she looked, but a boy never would. Randy would drop dead on the spot, if she asked him to fix Nicole up with one of his friends. One look at those ruffly dresses, and those awful Mary Jane shoes, and that would be it.

"Alison, you know that's impossible," Dana blurted out. "Have you taken a good look at her? I know you shouldn't judge people by their clothes, but really — she's like someone out of another century."

"Wait a minute," Faith interrupted. "Why can't we do something about her clothes? In fact, we could help her pick out some new things in Greenleaf today."

"We could," Dana agreed, a slow smile spreading over her face. "That's a fantastic idea." She started to get excited over the prospect of making over Nicole. It would be just like Pygmalion! And when they finished, Nicole would be bright, beautiful, and hip — the ideal American teenager.

Dana decided to call Randy on the way back from breakfast, and Faith coached her on what to say.

"Tell him she's kind of exotic," she suggested. "You know how boys always go crazy over foreign girls. They think they're going to look like the ones in the Italian movies. Long hair falling over one eye and terrific figures."

"Nicole — exotic?" They were standing at a pay phone in the dining hall while Dana fumbled in her pocket for change.

"Well . . . she's got long hair. And maybe we could steal her rubber bands so she can't put it in those awful braids."

"He'll kill me if I tell him she's exotic," Dana said, finally coming up with a quarter. "I'll have to tell him the truth. Sort of," she amended.

Faith giggled. "If you tell him the truth, he'll never come up with a blind date for her. You'll have to lie a little."

Dana groaned. "I'll just play it by ear." She dialed Randy's number, and was relieved when he answered on the first ring. Sometimes his brothers picked up the phone, and she always had to go through a lot of kidding before they put Randy on.

"Hi. Are we all set for tonight?" she said brightly. She felt a little nervous talking to him with Faith standing right there.

"Sure. Dinner at Pizza Pete's and a walk around the pond if it's not too cold." He sounded surprised. "Is anything wrong? You sound kind of funny."

"No, nothing's wrong," she said hurriedly. "I had an idea, though." She tried to put more enthusiasm in her voice than she really felt. "Do you remember me telling you about this new girl we have at Canby Hall? The French girl?"

"Oh yeah. Nicole, wasn't it? And a funny last name, like brick-bat."

"It's Brisbet. Anyway," she went on in a rush, "I was thinking it would be sort of fun if she came with us tonight."

"You were?" he said in an astonished voice. *He certainly isn't making this easy,* she thought. "Why would you want to do a thing like that? There's going to be six of us anyway, you and me, and Shelley and Tom, Faith and Johnnie —"

"I know," she said, "but I meant she could come with us . . . as part of a couple. As someone's date."

A long pause. "Whose?"

"Uh, well, I thought maybe you could handle that part for me. I figured you could get her a blind date."

"Oh." He didn't say anything for a long time, and for a moment, she thought they had been disconnected. At times, Randy could be maddeningly stubborn!

"You must know someone who's free tonight," she said hopefully. "Someone who'd like to go out with a . . . cute French girl?"

There was a long sigh from the other end of the phone. "Dana," Randy began, "you know how I feel about blind dates. I'd never go out on one myself, and I don't want to get involved setting one up. I think dating should be an 'every man for himself' sort of thing."

"Or every woman for herself," Dana corrected him.

"Right."

Dana was wondering what to say next when Faith passed her a note scribbled on an envelope. *Tell him she's alone in a strange country, etc.,* it said. Dana nodded.

"Randy, I'd never ask you to fix her up, but she's so . . . lonely. So vulnerable. Can you imagine what it would be like to be in a strange place where you can hardly speak the language?" That was exaggerating, of course, but this was no time to be technical. "And everything is so new to her," she pressed on. "No home or family or friends to fall back on. . . ." She knew that would get to him. He was really close to his family.

"All right, Dana," he said finally. "You don't have to get out the violins. If it's that important to you, I'll find someone for Nicole tonight. But don't expect a miracle," he said in a warning tone.

"Oh, I won't," Dana told him. *Don't you expect one either,* she added silently. She said her good-byes quickly and turned to Faith. "Well, it worked. We did it!" she said triumphantly.

Faith wrapped a bright red muffler around her neck, and said firmly, "Not yet we haven't." She grabbed Dana's arm and started for the door. "In case you've forgotten, our work is just beginning. We've got about eight hours to work a miracle on Nicole."

A miracle. It's funny, Dana thought, *that's just what Randy said.*

CHAPTER SEVEN

Faith, Dana, and Shelley spent Saturday afternoon with Nicole in downtown Greenleaf on a shopping expedition. They were wandering up and down the aisles at Pearson's, trying to find something that would catch the French girl's interest. So far, nothing had. Nicole was lagging far behind them, picking idly at belts and underwear, looking utterly bored.

"Americans all dress alike, no?" Nicole finally said. "You can't tell the boys from the girls." She fingered a pair of jeans and a studded leather jacket.

Shelley couldn't resist smiling. That was exactly what her father always said! But it seemed sort of funny to hear someone her own age saying it. "But isn't it just the same in your country, Nicole?" she said. "Doesn't everyone wear jeans and sweaters and tank tops?"

Nicole shrugged. "Not everyone. In France,

there are many girls who want to . . . look like girls." Faith and Dana exchanged a look, but Nicole didn't notice. "French girls, I think, are more feminine," Nicole went on. "For example, my mother would die if I came home in something like this." She pointed to a pair of dark green paratrooper's pants and a camouflage top and suddenly giggled.

"Why?" Dana asked, surprised. Her own mother encouraged her to wear the latest styles, and had just sent her a pair of tight satin pants she had picked up on a buying trip.

"I suppose she'd think I had just jumped out of a plane. Or maybe that I had joined the French foreign legion."

Faith started laughing, too. "We're not trying to dress you up in combat gear, Nicole. We just thought you might like to . . . uh. . . ." She turned to Dana.

"See what American kids are wearing," Dana finished for her. Faith shot Dana a grateful look. She'd have to remember to go slow with Nicole, she decided, or she'd risk hurting her feelings.

Nicole didn't say anything for a moment, and then retorted, "French girls never copy anyone else. We don't have to. We have our own style."

Dana stared at her. *Some style!* she thought glumly. Nicole was wearing a white ruffly blouse, a red pleated skirt that came to mid-calf, and impossible red patent leather shoes. What if she didn't get changed for the date tonight? Randy would kill her.

"Uh, Nicole," she said suddenly, "isn't there anything you'd like to try on? Just for fun," she pleaded.

To her amazement, Nicole swiftly pulled an expensive-looking black wool skirt off the rack. It was very slim, and had a row of buttons down one side. "This, I like," she said calmly. "And also, this. *C'est beau.*" She scooped up a pale apricot sweater with a plunging neckline. "I will try these on," she announced, and marched off to the dressing room.

"But that's not her style at all," Shelley protested. "Did you see what she picked —"

"Quiet," Dana said, nudging her in the ribs. "I don't care what she buys, just so she wears something besides that pleated skirt tonight."

A few minutes later, Nicole came out of the dressing room, her face expressionless. "I will take these," she said, and pulled some money out of her wallet.

Dana was so relieved that she offered to treat everyone to sodas at the Tutti-Frutti.

"You're on," Faith said fervently.

"Uh, count me out," Shelley said, glancing at her watch. If she hurried, she could just make it to the afternoon aerobics class at Heavenly Bodies.

"You're passing up a chocolate frosted?" Dana said incredulously. "You always said you'd kill for one!"

"I need to get back to the dorm and study," Shelley said weakly.

Dana frowned. "We're only going to be half an hour or so," she began.

"No, I really can't. It's those French verbs again — they're really murder," she added, making a face. "See you at dinner, gang!" She practically ran out of the store before her startled friends could ask her any more questions.

"Shelley's acting kind of weird, isn't she?" Faith said, as they waited with Nicole at the cash register. "First the disappearing act this morning, and now this."

"It's a little funny," Dana admitted. "But if she really wants to spend all her time studying, I guess we shouldn't discourage her. You know she's had problems with French before." Dana thought back to another time, when Shelley was so wrapped up with her boyfriend and her part in a school play, that her grades had dropped dangerously low. If her roommates hadn't stepped in and tutored her, she might have flunked out of Canby Hall.

If she's really spending all her time study-ing, Faith worried to herself.

Later that day, Shelley and Faith were in Room 407 getting ready for their evening out.

"Are you sure you and Johnny don't want to go to Pizza Pete's with us tonight?" Shelley asked. Johnny Bates was Faith's boyfriend from Greenleaf, and they saw each other nearly every weekend.

"Thanks, but we can't. His mother's fixing one of her special dinners, and she's having all the relatives over."

"Sounds serious," Shelley teased. "He wants to show you off to them."

"No, it's nothing like that," Faith said, giving her a shy smile. "I've met most of them already, and after all, Johnny met all my family when he came to D.C. to visit me."

"I used to go over to Paul's house all the time for dinner, too," Shelley said a little wistfully.

"Do you miss Paul a lot?" Faith asked. "I figured that Tom took up all your time and attention now."

"Paul still means a lot to me," Shelley said softly. "When I think about how long I've known him. I dated him ever since we were in grade school. Remember when I first got here? I was so lonely, I thought I wouldn't even make it through a day without him." She sighed and wriggled into a pair of gray wool pants and a black sweater.

"And now?"

Shelley shrugged, "Now I've got Tom, and well, nothing stays the same, does it?"

"And that's what makes life so interesting!"

Dana said, bursting in suddenly. She was wrapped in her big terry robe, and her long wet hair was streaming down her back. "That bathroom is freezing," she muttered. "I've got to get dressed fast before I turn into an icicle." She pulled open the closet doors and frowned. "Hey, what's everybody wearing tonight, anyway?" She looked questioningly at Faith. "Did you change your mind and decide to come with us? You look fantastic."

"She's having dinner with the Bates," Shelley said pointedly. "Can't you tell?"

"Ah ha! That sounds like the real thing."

"Don't you start in on me, too," Faith pleaded. She threw a camel hair coat over her red sweater and black velvet skirt. "Make sure you tell me what happens with Nicole's blind date, okay? I'll be dying from suspense all night."

"Just keep your fingers crossed," Dana said dryly. "If she turns up in those red shoes, you'll have a dead roommate on your hands. Don't forget, I listened to you and told Randy how cute she was. If she's dressed like Mary Poppins, he's going to murder me."

"Maybe Randy has a forgiving nature," Faith said with a grin.

As it turned out, Randy didn't need a forgiving nature after all. Nicole looked sensational. Not just average, not just cute, but really terrific, Dana decided.

In fact, the whole evening was full of surprises. When Casey knocked on the door a little after seven to say that Randy and Tom were in the lounge, Dana said quickly, "Thanks Casey. Would you do me a favor and tell Nicole that we'll come by her room for her in a couple of minutes?"

Casey had gotten a funny look on her face, and had said slowly, "She's doing fine, Dana. She's already in the lounge with the boys. And if I were you, I'd step on it."

"I wonder what that's all about?" Shelley said slowly. She looked in the mirror and tried to stifle a giant yawn. Maybe going to two aerobics classes in one day had been a mistake. She felt totally wiped out!

"I don't know," Dana said, tugging at a pair of cowboy boots, "but let's get down there and find out."

"What do you think she's wearing?" Shelley whispered as they hurried down the four flights of steps.

"Anything but those patent leather shoes," Dana said fervently. "I had really hoped I'd get a chance to talk to her and —"

Dana never got a chance to finish the sentence, because they had reached the first floor landing when Shelley suddenly gasped and pointed to the fireplace. "Is that Nicole?" she said in disbelief. "Over there with Randy and Tom?"

"I'm afraid it is," Dana said with a laugh.

"It looks like I didn't have anything to worry about after all." The two girls stood stock-still for a moment, staring at the remarkable transformation. Nicole had her back to them, but even from that angle, they could see the way the slim black skirt clung to her body, accentuating her shapely hips and legs. She had left the row of side buttons undone, and the skirt was open almost to the thigh, revealing black textured stockings.

"Well, at least she didn't wear the red patent leather shoes," Shelley said, eyeing Nicole's cut-out suede high heels.

"She certainly didn't," Dana agreed. "And she got rid of those braids, too."

"I noticed." Nicole's beautiful chestnut hair was hanging free, cascading down the back of her apricot sweater. The whole effect was sexy, sensational.

"And she doesn't seem as shy anymore," Dana said, sounding puzzled. Just as she spoke, Nicole laughed at something Randy had said, and reached out and touched his arm. Except she didn't just touch it, Dana noticed, she let her hand linger on his forearm before sliding it down to his wrist.

"Let's go," Shelley said. Tom was staring at Nicole like he had never seen a girl before, and she could hardly wait to get a look at her close up!

"Hi, gang," Dana said brightly. Nicole turned first, and Dana realized that her first impression was right. Nicole looked fabulous. She was wearing eye makeup, just a small amount of shadow and liner, but it made a big difference. Her brown eyes seemed to jump right out of her heart-shaped face, and a touch of blusher had brought out her high cheekbones. Her lips were touched with gloss, and they looked full and pouty, like Brooke Shields'.

"I see you've already met," Dana couldn't resist adding.

Randy looked a little embarrassed, and moved a few inches away from Nicole. "Hi, Dana, Shel. Nicole was just telling us about her country. Some of their customs are really different."

I'll bet, Shelley thought, wondering why Tom had such a silly smile on his face. There was an unbelievably long pause — which Tom and Randy spent staring at Nicole — when Dana finally said, "Where's Nicole's date?"

"Oh, that," Randy said casually, as if it really didn't matter one way or the other. "Well, to tell you the truth, I couldn't find just the right person for Nicole."

"But there's no reason the five of us can't go out together," Tom said eagerly. Too eagerly, Shelley thought.

"Oh no," Nicole said, in a charming French accent. "I would not want to . . . how do you say it? . . . be a fifth tire."

"A fifth wheel," Tom laughed. "You'd never be a fifth wheel, would she, Randy?"

"Never," Randy agreed. "You've got to come with us. We insist."

Nicole shrugged and said helplessly, "But the two of you are couples, and I am just a lone person —"

A lone wolf! Shelley added silently.

"Hey, you have to eat, Nicole. And the pizza is really great at Pete's. C'mon, you'll be doing us a favor." Randy smiled and put his arm around Nicole's shoulders in a brotherly way.

"Well, if you're sure," she said, ignoring Shelley and Dana. "I'll just go upstairs and get my coat." She flashed a dazzling smile and started for the stairs. Three boys coming in the front door stopped dead in their tracks to stare at her.

"You couldn't get *anyone* for her?" Dana said, the moment Nicole was out of earshot. "Why do I get the feeling you didn't try very hard?"

"That's not fair," Randy said indignantly. "I *did* try hard. . . ." She stared at him and he flushed. "Okay, maybe not as hard as I could have. But Dana, why didn't you tell me she was such a knock-out?" He glanced at Tom. "You said she was cute — she's more than cute. She's fantastic."

"I'm glad that you approve," Dana said. "But you should have called and told me you didn't have a date for her. Then I could have called it off."

"I thought you'd want her to come with us anyway," Randy said innocently. "After all, Dana, here she is in a strange country, and she can't even speak the language. . . ." It was Dana's turn to flush as she remembered using the same tactics on Randy. "I mean, well, it wouldn't be very neighborly of us not to invite her to come with us, would it?" he continued.

"I guess not," Dana said.

"It wouldn't be neighborly at all," Tom repeated solemnly, and Shelley felt like kicking him.

CHAPTER EIGHT

"All ready!" Nicole said in a charming
French accent. She did a little pirouette
in front of Randy and Tom, showing off a
black lamb's wool coat with velvet trim. She
looked very chic, very French, and Shelley
suddenly felt like a frump in her good winter
coat. She glanced at her watch, and cleared
her throat impatiently. At the rate they were
going, they'd never get out of the Baker
House lounge.

"Wonderful," Randy said, beaming. "I've
got the truck outside, and there's plenty of
room for you, Nicole."

"And I've got the car," Tom said quickly.
"With a new eight-track tape deck. I've even
got the new Elton John tape. I hear he's really
big in Europe."

"So take your pick," Randy said lightly.
"Who will it be?"

I don't believe this! Dana thought disgustedly. *In a minute, they'll be fighting over*

who's going to ride with Nicole.

Nicole promptly settled the argument. "Wait, I have a better idea," she said and playfully tugged at Randy's long cashmere scarf. "It is only a few kilometers to Greenleaf, no?"

"It's about a mile," Randy said. He smiled down at her. "I've never tried to figure it out in kilometers, but —"

"And it is a beautiful, starry night, no?" She put her head on one side and smiled winsomely at Tom.

"Uh, yeah, I think so," he gulped.

"Then . . . why don't we walk!" She threw her hands up in the air in a dramatic gesture. "You can give me the grand tour. First the campus, then Greenleaf."

"Yeah, we can walk. That's a great idea," Randy said. "How come we didn't think of it, Tom?" He was grinning from ear to ear.

"I don't know," Tom laughed. "Maybe it's just hard for guys to think straight around French girls."

"Ah no, no, that's very naughty to say," Nicole lisped. She wagged her finger teasingly at them, and then took one of each boy's arms. "So we go, no?"

"We go — definitely yes!" Randy said loudly. He turned to Dana and Shelley. "Ready, girls?"

"We're ready," Dana said with a tight-lipped smile. *For anything!* she added silently.

* * *

"What in the world has happened to Nicole?" Shelley whispered the moment they were out the door of the lounge. "She's got such a heavy accent tonight, I can hardly understand her."

"She doesn't care if *you* can understand her." Dana laughed shortly. "She knows that guys go crazy over girls with sultry foreign accents, and she's going to play it for all it's worth."

"The campus is very old," Randy was saying to Nicole, who was looking up at him adoringly. Somehow Nicole had managed to stay between Randy and Tom even on the narrow sidewalk, while Dana and Shelley were stumbling through snowdrifts, trying to keep up. Shelley wanted to pull Tom close to her and hold hands, but she wasn't sure how to go about it. She stared at Dana, watching for a cue, but for once, even the supercool New Yorker seemed at a loss.

Randy kept his eyes glued to Nicole, continuing his lecture. "In fact, it was founded by Horace Canby in 1896 —"

"1897," Dana interrupted. "And I hate to disappoint you," she said sweetly, "but we've already given Nicole a tour of the campus." *Two can play this game!* she thought.

"Oh, I'm sorry, Nicole," Randy said quickly. "I didn't mean to bore you with a lot of details you've already heard before."

Nicole laughed and disengaged her arm

from Tom's long enough to pat Randy's hand. "Bore me? *Jamais!* Never! With you, the history of the place comes alive. You have such a voice, the voice of an actor. I could listen to you forever."

If I have to listen to this *all night, I'll go nuts*, Dana thought. She was about to try to change the subject when Tom broke in smoothly.

"Actually, acting is my field more than Randy's." He ignored Randy's frown and went on. "I *am* an actor," he said, and waited for Nicole's reaction. He didn't have to wait long. Nicole's mouth dropped open, like someone who's just seen a vision, and she clasped her hands together.

"You are an actor?" she breathed. "Oh, I love actors. They are *magnifique*. Magnificent. Do you work on the stage, or in television?"

"Well, I'm still studying my craft," Tom said very seriously. "I've done the leads in practically all the school plays —"

"That's how we met," Shelley said pointedly. "At a school play. It was really funny, we —"

"And next year, I'm applying to Carnegie-Mellon," Tom rushed on, ignoring her.

"I'm impressed," Nicole said in a husky voice that must have taken hours to perfect. "I think in France we have more appreciation for the artist than you have here in America.

To be an actor in France is to be . . ." she paused and groped for a word ". . . a superman."

"A superman. Hey, I like that," Tom grinned. "I've got to learn a lot more about your country, Nicole," he said teasingly.

She smiled at him. "We have all night." Then she paused and turned to Randy. "There is so much we can teach each other."

After they had ordered at Pizza Pete's, Dana pulled Shelley into the ladies' room with her for a hurried consultation.

"France ten, U.S. zero," she said with a grimace. She began brushing her long brown hair more vigorously than was necessary.

"What are we going to do?" Shelley wailed. "Do you think she knows the effect she has on them?"

"I'm afraid she does," Dana said absently, as she added another layer of mascara.

Shelley stared into the mirror, and wished she had worn something more exciting. Her black turtleneck sweater and gray wool pants had seemed okay back in the dorm, but next to Nicole's dazzling outfit, they looked painfully dull.

"She's practically hypnotized them," she went on. "Did you see Tom's eyes? They were actually glazed. Why didn't you tell me that boys would react to her that way?"

"I'm as surprised as you are," Dana said.

"Remember, I'm the one who suggested she go shopping today." She shook her head. "And to think I was afraid she'd turn up in a ruffly dress and Mary Jane shoes."

"As it turned out, you had nothing to worry about," Shelley said sarcastically. "She managed to put together one of the most terrific outfits I've ever seen. And her hair," Shelley sighed. "It's gorgeous." Like most people with naturally curly hair, she longed for a yard of stick-straight, silky tresses.

"I suppose it's because she's so different from any other girls they've known," Dana said thoughtfully. She put the brush back in her purse and touched up her lip gloss. "I think that must be it. The lure of the unknown," she said with a grin. She took a final appraising look at her white sweater dress. *Not bad*, she thought. It clung in all the right places.

"C'mon," she said to Shelley, "let's get back out there and fight fire with fire."

"You mean we're going to speak French?"

"No," Dana said, giggling. "We're going to show them that American girls can be exciting, too."

Shelley took a last look in the mirror. By now, she absolutely hated her sweater and pants and vowed never to wear them again. "I hope you know what you're doing," she said in a little voice. "Because I don't feel very exciting."

* * *

"*Tete-a-tete,*" Nicole was saying in her lilting accent when they got back to the table. She had her face just inches from Randy's and was flirting outrageously. "It means head-to-head, I think." She smiled charmingly.

"It looks like nose-to-nose to me," Dana said acidly and squeezed into her seat. She glared at Nicole but the French girl returned her stare with an infuriating grin.

"Nicole was just saying it's funny the way French words keep cropping up in English," Randy explained. "Like tete-a-tete."

"And rendezvous," Nicole added. "And paramour." She giggled. "They are all romantic words. That is strange, no?" She was staring intently at Randy.

"Very strange," he agreed. "Well, you know what they say. French is supposed to be the language of love."

"Ah, *oui*. That I know very well." She flashed a dazzling smile at Tom, who flushed and turned a brilliant shade of red.

There was a long pause, and then Shelley spoke up. "We use a lot of other French words, too, like . . . croissant," she began thoughtfully. No one picked up on it, though, and her voice trailed off.

"Tell me about your ranch, Randy," Nicole said swiftly. "When I was little, I used to love to go to Western movies. I thought that all American men were cowboys." She laughed, and Randy and Tom joined in. If Nicole noticed that Dana and Shelley didn't crack a smile, she never let on. "I thought you were all very tall and strong and brave and carried . . . what do you call them? . . . six-shooters."

"Oh, that's all true, Nicole," Randy said, "everything but the six-shooters, anyway." He smiled. "My family owns a beautiful chunk of land way up high on a ridge. It's a real working ranch," he said proudly. "We've got some of the best-looking cattle you've ever seen, and we breed champion horses."

He didn't get a chance to say anything else because Nicole clapped her hands together ecstatically. "Horses! I would love to see them. It is permitted?" She cupped her chin in her hands and leaned close to him.

"Well, sure," Randy said slowly, and Dana thought he looked a little uncomfortable. "We'd love to have you come out to the ranch on a Saturday, wouldn't we, Dana? We can have lunch and ride one of the trails." He turned questioningly to Dana.

"It sounds good," she said tightly. "Of course, we'll have to wait for the weather to clear up. Everything's too wet right now. You said so yourself." She felt like kicking Randy under the table. From the look on his face, it was obvious that he wanted to take Nicole and rush out to the ranch that very minute.

The pizza came just then, and for a few blissful moments everyone was too busy eating to talk.

Dana studied Nicole as she took dainty bites of her pizza. *This has got to be the longest night of my life,* she thought despairingly. Nicole had wrapped the boys around her finger, and she was using every trick in the book to keep them.

Part of it was the voice, Dana decided. Nicole had put on a low, breathy voice, and managed to make plenty of "charming" mistakes with her English. When they got to Pizza Pete's, she pointed to the glasses of Coke and ice and said, "Ah, Coke on the stones. My favorite." The boys had practically killed themselves laughing, and Randy had said over and over, "Coke on the stones! I love it! Nicole, you're fantastic." The joke went on for several minutes, until Dana had put an end to it. "You mean 'on the rocks,' Nicole," she said sharply.

"Oh, really?" Nicole had said innocently. "I did not know."

Dana let her mind wander but she snapped back to attention when she heard a burst of masculine laughter. Nicole had obviously scored again.

"I don't see what I said that was so funny," she was saying plaintively. She turned to Dana. "You see, my napkin jumped off the table," she said, pointing to her napkin, which was lying on the floor.

"Jumped," Randy said. "That's cute. We've

got to remember that one." He grinned at Tom.

"Fell," Dana said coldly. "Your napkin fell off the table. Napkins can't jump." She let her breath out slowly and went back to her pizza.

"Fell, jumped. I can never remember the difference!" Nicole gave a little toss of her head that managed to rearrange the softly waving hair over one eye again. She pouted at Tom. "Tell me, Tom," she said, "do you think I will ever learn the English? Or am I hopeless case?" She smiled and then shook her finger at him. "Be truthful now. Like . . . a Boy Scout."

Tom laughed. "I used to be a Scout, as a matter of fact. Believe me, Nicole, your English is fantastic. You've got nothing to worry about. Right, Randy?"

Randy stared at her, obviously smitten. "Absolutely nothing," he agreed.

Dana met Shelley's eyes over the rim of her Coke glass. "I don't believe this!" she signaled silently to her friend.

Even the worst evenings come to an end, Dana thought gratefully, and she was glad when they finally got back to Baker House. She managed to get Randy alone, while Shelley, Tom, and Nicole decided to trudge around the lake.

"Are you sure you don't want to come with

us?" Nicole had said to Randy, but Dana had sweetly refused for both of them. She was determined to have her say with Randy.

"At last!" she said fervently. They were standing on the front porch of Baker House. It was a cool, clear night, and Dana wanted to take a walk around the lake — but not with Nicole. "I thought tonight would never end."

"Really?" Randy said in surprise. "What's wrong? I thought everything went very well. Nicole made some funny mistakes in English didn't she?" he added, smiling at the memory.

"Very funny," Dana said dryly. "But not as funny as the way you and Tom hung on her every word. Honestly, Randy, can't you see how phony she is? She speaks perfect English — she was trying to be cute, or flirtatious, or something." Dana paused. "And her clothes!"

"What's wrong with her clothes?" Randy grinned. "She looked pretty good to me. In fact, I can hardly wait to tell Jerry Stevens that he made the biggest mistake of his life tonight."

"Jerry Stevens?"

"He would have been Nicole's blind date tonight, but I couldn't talk him into it. I guess I wasn't persuasive enough."

"I wish you had been," Dana said grumpily. "I felt like a fifth tire, as Nicole said."

"That's silly," Randy laughed. "Hey, you're not jealous, are you?"

"Jealous? Of course not. But it wasn't much fun to watch the two of you make idiots of yourselves over Nicole," she said sharply.

"Well, what about you and Chris Canby? It's not much fun for me to think of you going out with that guy."

"We're just friends, Randy. And besides, Chris and I don't drag you along with us and then ignore you for a whole night."

Randy's face tightened. "It was your idea, Dana." His voice was light, but she knew he was annoyed. "If you recall, I was against the idea from the start. Blind dates never work out, remember?"

"After this, I'll believe you," she retorted. She stared stonily out at the snow-covered walks and buildings.

Randy laughed softly. "Nicole's not with us now," he said, moving closer to her. Dana stared at him and didn't answer. "Remember that rule about no kissing on campus?" he went on.

"Of course I do," she said flatly. "It's one of Canby Hall's oldest traditions."

He grinned at her, his face half-hidden in shadows. "Let's break it."

CHAPTER NINE

"It sounds awful," Faith said the next day at breakfast. She listened sympathetically as Shelley and Dana filled her in on Nicole and the episode at Pizza Pete's. "The funny thing is, I really had bad vibes about last night. I even told Johnny that I was worried about the way things might be going."

"It was beyond my worst dreams," Dana said feelingly. "Nicole was just impossible, wasn't she, Shelley?"

Shelley nodded. "She did a three-hundred-and-sixty degree turn, that's for sure. It was just like Dr. Jekyll and Mr. Hyde. She wasn't anything like we expected. She got rid of the ruffly dress and the patent leather shoes, and she was —" She turned to Dana for help.

"She was a knock-out," Dana said flatly. "And an unbelievable flirt. I think if I'd been gone from the table one minute longer, she would have been sitting in Randy's lap." She took a tentative bite of her oatmeal. Patrice

Allardyce always insisted that hot cereals be included on the breakfast menus in the winter months. The only trouble, Dana thought wryly, was that the cooks always served them stone cold! She sighed and pushed away her plate.

"Maybe things would have been better if Randy had come through with that blind date, like he promised," Faith said thoughtfully. "Then Nicole could have concentrated on her own date, and not tried to grab anyone else's."

"No, that wouldn't have helped," Dana said. "There's something funny about Nicole. She doesn't think she's a success unless she fascinates every guy within a hundred yards."

Everyone was quiet for a few minutes then, lost in their own thoughts. Sunday was a quiet, relaxed kind of day at Canby Hall, and most of the girls lingered in the dining hall after breakfast, talking, drinking tea, and reading the paper.

Suddenly a laughing voice broke the silence. "Hey, what's wrong with you guys? You'd think you were in a library!" There was a familiar ripple of laughter, and Dana blinked and looked up. Casey Flint. "Here's something to cheer you up," Casey added merrily. "They just put out a tray of sweet rolls and I grabbed a whole bunch for us." She grinned and plunked a tray of Danish pastry on the middle of the table. "We won't have to starve to death after all."

"They look great," Faith said, grabbing a cheese Danish. "I'll get refills on the tea and hot chocolate," she added, reaching for the cups.

"What's everybody up to this morning?" Casey peered at Dana and Shelley and laughed. "I've never seen you two look so down in the dumps." She peeled off her poncho and sat down, revealing a bright purple T-shirt with a "Don't Ask" button pinned near the shoulder.

"We're just re-hashing our dates last night," Shelley explained.

"But I think we about covered the topic," Dana said. "Let's just chalk it up to experience, and forget about it." She smiled at Shelley. "There's no sense in ruining Casey's breakfast."

"Oh yeah, the blind date," Casey said slowly. "It was that bad?"

Dana nodded. "You don't want to know." She bit into a raspberry Danish and smiled. Pastries were the only thing the Canby Hall cooks couldn't ruin. They had them delivered fresh from a bakery in Greenleaf and served them right out of the box. "How come you're looking so pleased with yourself? Is there something you're not telling us?"

Casey laughed. "There sure is," she said teasingly. "While all of you were out with your boyfriends last night, I had a heart-to-heart with Alison. We split a pizza and guess what she told me?" She waited a second and then blurted out, "Fort Lauderdale — it's on!"

"We know," Faith said casually. "Alison gave us the word yesterday morning. I hope everybody's still planning on going."

"Oh," Casey said, a little disappointed. "Here I thought I had the news scoop of the century."

"I called Mom last week," Dana said. "She thought it was fantastic, but she wanted me to check with Dad. I was going to anyway," she said quietly. "I knew she was a little short of cash, so I was going to ask him for the fare."

"And —" Faith asked.

"He came through," Dana said flatly. "In fact, he encouraged me to go." She gave a harsh laugh. "Ever since he married Eve, he's been on a guilt trip. I could ask for the moon, and he'd probably come through with the money."

"Well, who else is in and who's out?" Casey continued. "Shelley, I can tell from the big grin on your face that you're going."

"It's that obvious?" Shelley teased her.

"It sure is. You just can't keep a secret, Shelley. We can read you like a book," Dana told her.

"Well, you're absolutely right," Shelley agreed. "I'm definitely going. In fact, I'll be the first one on the beach! I made a deal with my mom. She'll lend me the money now and I'll save up and pay her back."

"That's great!" Casey said.

"I don't believe it," Dana said suddenly.

"What?" Shelley said, craning her neck to see what Dana was staring at.

"Miss Crepe Suzette herself," Dana said irritably. "And there's Pamela bringing up the rear."

"That's my cue, gang," Casey said, springing to her feet. "A glutton for punishment, I'm not."

"But you haven't had breakfast," Shelley reminded her.

Casey scooped up two sweet rolls and wrapped them in a napkin. "They'll taste better at Baker House," she said in a low voice. "If you're smart, you'll do the same thing."

She disappeared before Nicole and Pamela reached the table. "Allo," Nicole said cheerfully, as if the previous evening had never happened.

"She must have amnesia," Shelley whispered to Dana.

"Or she thinks we do," Dana said grimly. "Hello, Nicole," she said in a frosty voice.

The French girl didn't seem at all put off by her tone, and sat down next to Shelley. "There's a seat here for you, Pamela," she said cheerfully. She didn't have a trace of an accent.

"I see your English has improved," Dana said drily.

"What's that?" Nicole said, puzzled.

"Nothing."

There was a painfully long pause, and Pamela volunteered, "Well, at least the Florida thing is on."

Faith, Dana, and Shelley exchanged a quick look. The one thing they had counted on was a week-long escape from Pamela and Nicole.

"Is the word already out?" Faith said, surprised.

Pamela smiled, showing her perfect white teeth. "Alison put up a notice on the bulletin board over there." She pointed to the lobby at the front of the cafeteria. "It gives the dates and the prices, where we'll stay, that kind of thing. And there's some permission slips for our parents to sign."

Where we'll stay, Shelley thought glumly. Pamela *was* going to go. *I wonder what changed her mind?*

She was trying to get up her nerve to ask, when Pamela said suddenly, "It will be so wonderful for Nicole." Of course, that was it, Shelley realized with a start. Pamela was determined to get friendly with Nicole, and what better way than a school trip?

"Why do you think it will be so wonderful?" Dana said acidly. "I thought that Florida was a giant swampland to you. At least that's what you said the last time we talked."

"Well," Pamela hedged, twisting a lock of blonde hair round and round, "I think you misunderstood me. Actually, I was comparing it to the Riviera. *La Cote d'Azur,*" she said with a quick smile at Nicole. "And of course, there *is* no comparison," she added with a world-weary sigh.

"Oh, I see," Dana said as she watched Pamela sipping her coffee. She no longer took it black, but added plenty of hot milk, in the French fashion. *Anything to keep up with Nicole,* Dana thought, amused.

She was dressed elegantly, expensively, completely wrong for Sunday morning in a boarding school cafeteria. Her tan leather pants fit her like a second skin, and her gold-flecked sweater was just peek-a-boo enough to make people look twice.

Dana was dying to see what Nicole had on, but the French girl sat there, bundled up to her chin in a coat and muffler, complaining about the cold.

"I thought you'd be used to the cold. With all the skiing you do and all," Shelley said to her.

Nicole shrugged. "The cold here seems different. I don't know why. Even on the coldest days at our chalet at Gstaad, I don't feel like this."

Pamela shot her a puzzled look and said slowly, "I thought your chalet was at Chamonix."

"Yes, it is," Nicole said hurriedly. "The new one is. But the old one — the one I spent so much time at — was at Gstaad. Whenever I think of skiing, I think of going there."

"Oh," Pamela said. Dana thought she saw something flicker in those deep blue eyes, but she couldn't be sure, and the moment passed.

"Do you want me to get some permission slips off the bulletin board for us?" Faith asked in a dispirited way.

"We can get them on the way out," Dana said absently, staring into her coffee cup. "There's no hurry."

Knowing Pamela was going had cast a cloud over the whole project, Faith thought, annoyed. And she had been counting on having the time of her life. After all, she was spending her own money going on the trip — money she had been saving for two whole years. She always felt funny about spending money on herself when things were so tight at home. Since her father died, her mother had had to watch every penny. In fact, her sister Sarah, who was at Georgetown, always joked that Mom could write a book called "One Hundred Ways to Serve Spaghetti." Sarah's school expenses were high, in spite of her partial scholarship, and Faith knew that she hadn't bought herself a new blouse or sweater in months. But when she'd talked it over with her mother on the phone Mrs. Thompson had said, "Honey, we all need something to look forward to. And I think going to Florida would be the best thing in the world for you — I really do." When Faith had expressed guilt about blowing the money just on herself, her mother had said warmly, "You worked hard to earn it, Faith, so now it's time to enjoy it."

It wasn't until they were back in 407 after breakfast, that she decided to bring up the subject with Dana. "Are you guys having second thoughts about Fort Lauderdale?" she said tentatively.

"I guess not," Dana said. She flashed a wan smile. "If I don't seem like a ball of fire, I guess it's because I'm still really annoyed at the way Randy acted last night. Like a total idiot!"

"You can include Tom," Shelley said wryly. "Make that two total idiots!"

"But you're not thinking of canceling out because Pamela and Nicole are going, right?"

"No way," Dana said firmly. "I'm not going to let them spoil our good time." She looked at Shelley. "Besides, I think the two of us could use a change of scenery, right? Maybe new boyfriends," she laughed. "Even temporary ones."

"You're absolutely right," Shelley agreed. She glanced out the window and saw that a light snow had started to fall. If she didn't leave for Heavenly Bodies soon, she'd be wading through snowdrifts in soggy jeans. "Hey, I've got to go," she said quickly. "My

term paper awaits." She picked up a loose-
leaf notebook and headed for the door.

"Wait up," Dana said casually. "I'll walk
you. I need to go to the library, too."

"Sure," Shelley gulped. Now what was she
going to do? What was that saying that her
English teacher was always quoting? "Oh
what a tangled web we weave, when first we
practice to deceive. . . ." Then she had an
idea. "But I have to stop by Addison first. I
need to get some notes from Martha Hilde-
brande."

"Oh," Dana said, pulling on her boots.
"Well, maybe you should just go ahead. I'm
going to be a few minutes, and I don't want
to keep you waiting."

"Okay," Shelley said gratefully. She bolted
for the door before Dana could change her
mind. "See you later, guys."

"I still say she's acting weird," Faith said
thoughtfully. "So nervous and jumpy, like
something's really bothering her."

"Don't worry about Shel. She's probably
just annoyed at Tom. Once she gets some of
that Florida sunshine, she'll forget all her
troubles." She opened her Spanish book and
closed it. "You know I really don't feel like
going to the library. What do you say we get
Alison and go into Greenleaf for lunch this
afternoon? I can't face that cafeteria again
today."

"Great idea," Faith said. She was idly

staring out the window, watching the snow turn the shrubs into ice cream sculptures. "Now that's really strange," she said softly.

"What is?"

"You're not the only one who doesn't feel like going to the library today. Shel is heading in the opposite direction." She watched Shelley's jacket disappear down the winding path past the science building.

"She's going to Addison first," Dana said. "Don't you remember? She has to get some notes."

"Nope. No way." Faith shook her head and her eyes met Dana's. She looked outside again and did a double take. "She's heading away from the library and away from Addison. In fact . . . this is really crazy . . . but I think she's going to Greenleaf."

"Greenleaf? Why would she do a thing like that? And why would she lie about it?"

Faith shrugged. "I don't know, Dana. But I wonder if maybe we should try to find out."

CHAPTER TEN

I'm glad you guys suggested this," Alison said later that afternoon. "I was getting a little stir-crazy staying in The Penthouse all day."

It was three-thirty, and she was splitting a giant mushroom and sausage pizza with Faith and Dana at Pizza Pete's. The place was nearly empty, since the lunch crowd had cleared out, and it was much too early for dinner. They were sitting by the window, watching the falling snow blanket the Greenleaf streets, happy to be inside the cozy little restaurant.

"I wonder what you call a meal like this?" Dana said idly. She took a bite of pizza and gave a contented sigh. "If it's in between breakfast and lunch you call it brunch, but if it's in between lunch and dinner it must be—"

"It must be escape," Faith joked. "Escape from Canby Hall cooking."

Alison smiled. "I'm surprised Shelley didn't

come with us," she said, helping herself to the frosty pitcher of Coke on the table. "I've never seen her pass up pizza before."

"She had a lot to do," Dana said blithely.

"So she said," Faith muttered.

Alison raised her eyebrows. "Why do I get the feeling there's something you're not telling me? Shelley's not in some kind of trouble, is she?" She leaned back in her chair with a worried expression on her face. "Because if there's anything I should know about —"

"She's just spending some time by herself lately," Dana said reassuringly. She grinned at her roommate. "Faith likes to make a mystery out of everything, but I really don't think there's anything wrong. After all, everybody needs some time alone. I've heard you say that yourself, Alison. Just because the three of us share a room together, doesn't mean we have to know every little detail of each other's lives."

"Yes, I guess you're right," Alison agreed. "So, is everybody pretty well set on Florida?" she asked suddenly. "Michael and I want to go ahead and make the hotel reservations. If we book early, we can get a better deal."

"Everybody I talked to got their permission slips in the mail right away," Faith said.

"Good." Alison drew a design on the red-checkered tablecloth with her fork, and said thoughtfully, "Let's see, I've got ten girls from Baker, six from Addison, and four from Charles. If everyone comes through with their money and permissions, that will make a pretty good number. At least it's enough to get group rates at the hotel."

"Where are we staying?" Dana asked. "I forgot to pick up one of those sheets you typed."

"I've got an extra one with me," Alison said, digging into her purse. It was a hand-woven Mexican satchel, and Alison had stuffed it to overflowing. "The Sand Dunes," she said, handing Dana the photocopied sheet. "I picked it because it's right on the water, and it's near all the restaurants and shops. Also, they take student groups," she added wryly. "You'd be surprised how many hotels down there refuse to."

"Really?" Faith asked. "Why's that?"

"Because they've had so much trouble with kids," Alison explained. "Sometimes groups of teenagers check into hotels with no chaperones, and there can be a lot of problems."

"You mean all those wild movies about Fort Lauderdale are true?" Dana said innocently. "Thousands of college kids and crazy parties, and people ending up in the swimming pool at two in the morning?"

"I'm sure the movies exaggerate things quite a bit," Alison said seriously. "In any case, it won't affect us one way or another, right? I'm counting on everybody to behave."

She gave a little laugh. "Just remember, if anything happens, you'll be looking for another housemother, because P.A. will have my head on a platter. She's still not crazy over the whole thing."

"C'mon, you know you can count on us," Dana said. "I was just kidding you." She paused and glanced at Faith. "I hate to bring up unpleasant subjects, but did Pamela and Nicole ask for permission slips?"

"They sure did. They wanted to get them in the mail right away, since they have to go to Europe." She looked at Dana very seriously. "Shelley told me you two had a pretty disastrous Saturday night with Nicole," she said softly. "Is it going to be a problem for you if she comes on the trip?"

"No," Dana said shortly. "I'm sure she'll be spending most of her time with Pamela anyway. The two of them have become really close, haven't you noticed?"

Alison nodded. "I was amazed. I thought that Pamela was the last person in the world Nicole would want to be friendly with. Then I figured it out." She paused. "They're impressed by each other."

"That's it, exactly," Faith agreed. "Pamela loves the idea of being friendly with someone from Paris, someone who skis in the right places and has yachts and chalets."

"And Nicole likes being friendly with the daughter of a movie star," Dana suggested.

"That's almost as good as being royalty, to some people."

"I thought Nicole *was* royalty," Faith said. "At least that was the story going around when she first got here. Is it true, Alison?"

"I don't know. I heard something about that, too, but Nicole is awfully vague about her parents."

"She makes it clear that they're filthy rich, though," Dana said sarcastically. "And Pamela eats up every word." She reached for another piece of pizza and sighed happily. "You know, this has got to be the best pizza I've ever had. And we even got it the way Shel likes it, with extra cheese. Darn it, I told her she should have come with us."

Dana happened to glance out the window just then, and she could have sworn she saw Shelley — or someone with the same jacket — disappearing down a side street. She craned her neck, and pulled the curtain aside to get a better look, but it was too late. Shelley — or her look-alike — had already turned the corner, and was out of sight.

"Anything wrong?" Alison asked curiously.

Dana shook her head. "No, I just wanted to see if it was going to start snowing again. The sky looks funny over in the west, doesn't it?"

They spent the next few minutes discussing the weather, and whether or not they'd be able to escape a snowstorm on the way back to Canby Hall. Dana was glad she hadn't said anything about spotting the girl in the coat, because she didn't want Faith to make a big deal out of it, and try to play amateur detective again.

At that very moment, a few blocks away, Shelley was wishing she'd never heard of aerobics. Or shin splints, or "pecs," or lateral abdominal muscles. It was a whole new world, a new vocabulary, to her. She felt lost, they way she did in French class sometimes, when she realized that everyone else was miles ahead of her.

She glanced around the exercise room at Heavenly Bodies. It was funny, but you could barely tell the students from the teachers — at least in the advanced classes. To Shelley all the girls seemed tall and skinny and energetic, in their rainbow-colored leotards and striped leg-warmers.

And they were tireless. They were in the middle of an aerobic dance routine, and Shelley was puffing her way through a combination of turns and stretches to the thumping beat of Michael Jackson. She couldn't understand what was wrong. All the other girls made it look so effortless, but she turned the wrong way twice and slammed into the wall. By the time she managed to rejoin the group, they were whirling to the center of the floor for a grand finale finish. She limped sadly to catch up with them, and felt like an idiot.

Later, in the changing room, she saw Cindy, who was wearing sparkly violet tights with her pink leotard. She looked like a show girl.

"You're looking good," Cindy said cheerfully. Shelley felt a silly rush of pleasure, and then remembered that Cindy told *everyone* they were looking good, even enormously fat Mrs. Huggins who had come to two classes and then dropped out of sight forever.

"Do you still think I can be bikini material?" Shelley said shyly. She always felt a little awed by Cindy — a little overpowered by her china-doll face, her pink-and-white perfection.

Cindy threw a towel around her neck and stared at her. "Well, of course you can. It just takes plenty of practice. Don't forget, I've been at this for years." Cindy absently grabbed her ankle and raised her leg straight up over her head. She held it steady, with her knee grazing her ear, as if it were the most natural position in the world. The first time Shelley saw her do it, her jaw dropped, but she soon learned that it was all part of an elaborate "cool-down" period that Cindy went through.

"You know, Shelley," she went on in her silky voice, "you might want to think seriously about coming here more often. We have some students who take class twice a day."

Twice a day! Shelley was using up every penny of her allowance money the way it was.

She wasn't a "regular" member of the club, since it cost hundreds of dollars to join. She had signed up as a "walk-in" and bought a little pink card that was good for eight visits at a time.

"Gee, I don't know," she began hesitantly. "I can barely keep up with all my school work now. And I can't cut my classes. . . ." Her voice trailed off, and Cindy looked at her, unconvinced.

"Well, I know what you can do!" she said brightly. "How about if you start coming in for our Early Bird Special? We start class at six-thirty in the morning. It's a short version of our regular workout, and you can be out of here by seven sharp."

"Six-thirty?" Shelley said weakly. She wondered if she could drag her tired body to Greenleaf at that hour. She'd have to get up at ten of six, pull on some clothes, and leave the dorm at ten after. Maybe she could sleep in her leotard. Then she could save time by not having to change.

"When was it you said you were going to Florida?" Cindy prompted. She had released her ankle and was doing graceful side splits on the floor, pressing her forehead to her knee.

Shelley watched her, fascinated. The girl was a human pretzel. "Uh, about another two weeks," she mumbled.

Cindy looked up, all smiles. Her skin was

glowing, her eyes were shining; she wasn't even sweating or out of breath.

"Only two weeks! Time's running out," she said merrily. Before Shelley could reply to this heartening statement, Cindy abruptly flipped over, and arched her body into a shoulder stand. "Think about it," she urged. "You still need a lot of work on your thighs."

Shelley glanced down involuntarily at the offending thighs. They did look a little big — almost like country hams — in spite of her efforts. But six-thirty! Still, if there was a chance of looking like Cindy. . . .

"I'll think about it," Shelley said weakly to Cindy's toes.

Shelley left Heavenly Bodies in a depressed state. After seeing the other girls, and especially Cindy, she wondered if she was really making progress at all. She was trudging along Main Street in Greenleaf, bone-tired, when she heard a familiar voice.

"Shel! Hop in!"

She grinned when she saw Tom peering out of his father's car, and then she remembered she was supposed to be mad at him. After all, he had acted like a monster the night before.

"No thanks, I'll walk," she said tightly.

"What? You're kidding," he said incredulously. He smiled good-naturedly at her. "Do you know what the wind chill factor is today?" He slowed the car to a crawl, and was keeping pace with her. "You'll freeze before you ever make it back to Canby Hall."

He was still smiling, and Shelley realized with a start that he had no idea she was angry with him. The made her even more furious. *Boys can really be annoying,* she thought. It's really frustrating to be mad at a boy — half the time he doesn't even know it.

"Hey, you better hop in. You're going to freeze," he was saying. A few cars were already lined up behind him, blasting their horns.

"Oh, all right!" Shelley said irritably. She stepped into a pile of slush, and opened the car door. She was careful to sit as close to the door as possible, so he wouldn't get the wrong idea. There was no sense in being subtle — she'd have to hit him over the head to let him know how she felt.

He reached over and flipped the heater on high. "That's better, isn't it?" he said pleasantly. "I figured you must have a death wish. It's below freezing, you know. Pneumonia weather, as my mother would say."

"Would that matter to you?" she snapped.

"What?" he said absently, fiddling with the dial on the radio.

"If I got pneumonia," she said coldly. "Would it matter that much to you if I got pneumonia?" she asked, with heavy patience.

They had stopped at a red light, and he looked at her in amazement. "Gee, Shelley, what's wrong? You don't seem like you're in a great mood. Did something happen at school?"

He really could be remarkably thick, she decided. "Tom," she said slowly, "don't you remember anything about last night?"

"Last night?"

"The French bombshell," she said sarcastically. "I assume you do remember a certain girl named Nicole."

"Oh yeah," he said, suddenly understanding. "That was fun. We'll have to get together again sometime."

The five of us? she felt like asking. She glanced over at Tom, who was concentrating on the winding road back to Canby Hall.

"It was a fun night," he said cheerfully.

She gave up. "Yeah, a lot of fun," she said. "I can hardly wait to do it again." She settled back against the seat, grateful for the warm air swirling around her legs. She supposed she should have refused to get in the car, but Tom was right — it was freezing out. And the car was so warm and soft, like a pink cloud, she thought dreamily. . . .

The next thing she knew, Tom was shaking her roughly awake. "Hey, we're here," he said, laughing.

She sat up and blinked. They were parked in front of Canby Hall. "I must have dropped off," she said groggily.

"You sure did," he said, walking around

to open her door. "I've never seen anybody fall asleep so fast. You must have been wiped out." He looked at her thoughtfully. "Have you been up late or something?"

"Studying," she said quickly. "I've been spending a lot of time in the library. You can ask Dana," she added idiotically.

Tom laughed. "I believe you, Shelley." When they got to the front door of Baker House, he paused. "Think I could come in for a few minutes? I sure could use a cup of something hot to drink."

Shelley hesitated. All she really wanted to do was go up to 407 and collapse on the bed. Still, Tom had given her a ride home, and it would look strange if she said no.

"Sure," she said, forcing some enthusiasm into her voice. "That sounds good to me, too." With any luck, he'd leave as soon as he had some coffee.

CHAPTER ELEVEN

The lounge at Baker House was warm and inviting, and Tom sank gratefully onto a low, chintz-covered bench in front of the fireplace. It was always crowded on Sunday afternoons, the day traditionally reserved for visitors, and a lot of the girls entertained their boyfriends or parents. Patrice Allardyce had instructed the dorm mothers to always keep a supply of drinks and snacks available, and Alison had donated a giant coffee urn she found at a yard sale. Shelley walked over to the snack table to get them some coffee.

"You missed a good pizza," Dana said, coming up behind her quietly.

Shelley jumped guiltily. "I, uh, just wasn't hungry," she said quickly. "Besides, I had too much to do." She glanced around the room, eager to change the subject. "Did Randy come over to see you this afternoon?"

Dana nodded. "I was just settling down for a boring round of algebra when he called.

We thought we'd have some coffee, and then maybe take a walk around the lake." She laughed. "I was going to really let him have it after the way he acted the other night, but it's hard to stay mad at him. In fact, I don't think he even realized that he was making such a fuss over Nicole —"

She broke off suddenly, and a shocked look crossed her face. "The rat!" she hissed softly. "She's at it again."

"Who?" Shelley said, pouring coffee carefully into two styrofoam cups. Dana grabbed her arm angrily, and the coffee sloshed over the table. "Hey, what's with you today?" Shelley started to protest. "Look what you made me do!"

"Forget the coffee," Dana whispered tensely, her fingers still digging painfully into Shelley's forearm. "Take a look at what's going on over by the window."

Shelley turned slowly, wondering if Dana had lost her mind. And then she spotted Nicole.

"Holding court," was the first thing that that came into her mind. There was something regal about the way that Nicole was perched in front of the leaded windows, surrounded by her adoring subjects. There were half a dozen boys sitting at her feet, including Randy and Tom, who were hanging on her every word.

She looks sensational, Shelley thought dully.

Nicole was wearing a black and white alpine sweater with tight black ski pants and fur-topped black boots. Her hair was hanging loose down her back, and she wore tiny pearl earrings.

"She's snared them again!" Dana said incredulously. "Let's get over there. I don't want to miss a word of this."

Shelley grabbed the coffee and doughnuts and hurried after Dana, who was marching purposefully across the room.

"I'll bet she's putting on that French accent again," Dana whispered over her shoulder. "This time, I've had it with her, I really have!"

They approached the group, just as Nicole was finishing telling what seemed like a riotously funny story. "And so I said to him, why do you want me to go on a wild duck chase?" She gave an innocent smile, and threw her hands helplessly in the air. "A wild duck chase! You Americans say such funny things." This brought an appreciative burst of male laughter.

Dana smiled thinly at Shelley. "What did I tell you?" she muttered. "She's at it again."

"You mean a wild goose chase, Nicole," someone said in a throaty voice. This was followed by an indulgent chuckle and Shelley was surprised to see that it came from Pamela. She was sitting in one of the big wing chairs, a little to the left of the window

seat, and was smiling good-naturedly at
Nicole. Amazingly, she didn't seem to resent
her being the center of attention.

Which was totally out of character, Dana
thought grimly. Then she remembered what
Alison had said. Nicole and Pamela were
birds of a feather. They'd be nice to each
other, as long as there was something in it
for each of them.

"Here's your coffee," she said loudly to
Randy, thrusting the paper cup at him.

"Sure. Thanks," he said, and didn't even
bother looking at her. "Tell the story about
the napkin, Nicole. You know, when you
went out for pizza with us." He turned to
the group and said confidently, "Wait till you
hear this. You'll crack up."

Dana and Shelley exchanged a glance while
Nicole recounted the story of the napkin
"jumping" from the table in Pizza Pete's.

"Do you believe it? They're all falling for
it," she said in a low voice to Shelley. "Guys
are so gullible."

"I've given up on Tom," Shelley said wearily. "I might as well be invisible when
Nicole's around."

Nicole had just finished the napkin story,
when Renee Rivette, a foreign exchange student, walked through the lounge. Renee
wasn't the friendliest girl in the world, and
Dana was surprised when she made it a point
to greet Nicole.

"*Bonjour*," she said simply, then added, "*Ca va?*"

"*Oui, bien*," Nicole replied a little uncertainly. She was obviously surprised by Renee's sudden interest in her.

"I hear you're going to Florida with us," Renee said.

"Yes, I am," Nicole said. She smiled at everyone. "My first time to visit . . . how do you say? . . . where the boys are!" She pushed up the sleeves on her sweater, and Dana noticed that she was wearing half a dozen silver bracelets. *Whoever's helping her with her wardrobe is doing a great job,* Dana thought ironically. *She's come a long way from ruffly dresses and headbands.*

The silver bracelets jangled as Nicole ran a hand through her long, dark hair. "Many of us here in Baker House are going. Almost everyone, I think."

"You're going to Florida?" Randy blurted out to Dana. She was pleased to see that he seemed upset. At least it had shaken him up enough so that he tore his eyes away from Nicole.

"That's right," she said casually. "Alison and Michael Frank are taking about twenty of us to Fort Lauderdale over semester break."

"When did all this happen?" Tom said, whirling around. "You never said a word about it," he added accusingly to Shelley.

"Oh, it's been in the planning stages for

a few weeks," Shelley said lightly. "It's certainly no secret, is it, Dana?"

"Of course not," Dana said, picking up her cue. "No secret at all," she said, grinning from ear to ear. "I think everyone needs a change of scenery now and then, don't you?" She smiled sweetly at Tom and Randy. "It gives you a fresh perspective on everything."

"Well, I still think it's kind of funny neither one of you ever said a word about it," Tom groused. He exchanged a look with Randy. "I guess girls like to keep secrets, huh?"

"It's part of our charm," Dana said teasingly. She turned her attention back to Nicole, who seemed suddenly to have lost some of her assurance. She was sitting tensely on the edge of the window seat, twisting her napkin in her tiny hands.

"Where does your family come from?" Renee was saying. "You're Parisian, I suppose?" Renee stared at her with her sharp, dark eyes.

"Yes, of course, we're Parisian. What else?" Nicole laughed a little nervously and jumped to her feet.

"My family, also. What *arrondissement* do you live in?" Renee persisted.

"The fifth," Nicole replied swiftly. "We live in the fifth *arrondissement*." She seemed very uncomfortable, as if she was ready to bolt from the room, Dana thought. "I must go study now," Nicole said quickly, "the snap quiz awaits."

"*Pop* quiz," Dana muttered through gritted teeth.

Nicole gave a final dazzling smile, and disappeared up the stairs with Pamela. Renee turned to stare at them with a puzzled expression on her face.

When she saw Shelley and Dana looking at her, she shrugged. "The fifth *arrondissement*." she said thoughtfully. "She's a strange girl." She walked away before anyone could respond to this surprising announcement.

"You said it," Shelley said fervently. She turned to Tom and Randy. "Now that we have your undivided attention, how about a quick walk around the lake before dinner?" She tucked her arm through Tom's. It was nice not to have to compete with Nicole for his attention.

"Good idea," Randy said. He stared at Dana. "You can tell us all about this Fort Lauderdale trip. I think Tom and I have been kept in the dark long enough."

"Yeah, how are we supposed to get along without you for a week?" Tom said plaintively.

Shelley smiled at Dana as she shrugged into her coat. "Nothing like a little absence to make the heart grow fonder," she whispered mischievously.

* * *

The next two weeks passed in a blur of frenzied activity. Even though Alison urged every one to concentrate on studying hard for midterms, it was impossible not to get caught up in what Dana called Florida Fever. There were almost day-to-day bulletins from Alison ("remember to pack plenty of sun-screen") and a brisk reminder from P.A. that they would be expected to act like "Canby Hall girls" at all times.

The girls in 407 saw very little of Pamela and Nicole during this time — or even of each other — since there was so much to do. Alison was like the calm in the eye of a storm, keeping track of money and permission slips, fielding phone calls from worried parents, and consulting with Michael Frank about the best way to keep twenty teenage girls occupied in southern Florida.

Almost miraculously, everything fell into place. Hotel reservations were confirmed, airline tickets were paid for, and suddenly it was The Night Before.

"I can't believe we're really going tomorrow morning," Shelley said, looking at the half-packed suitcases strewn all over the floor in 407. They had eaten an early dinner, so they'd have plenty of time to wash their hair and finish packing. Everything was taking much longer than they had expected, though, and Shelley was dismayed when she noticed that it was ten-thirty.

"Panty hose," Dana said flatly. "That's what I've forgotten." She dove into her dresser drawer, and came up empty-handed. "And not one clean pair!"

"You've still got time to wash some," Faith suggested. "But you really should step on it. I've got the feeling that Alison is going to appear around midnight, and remind us to get some sleep."

"I'm too excited to sleep anyway," Shelley said. "This is the third big trip of my life." She was sitting on the edge of her bed, filing her finger nails, dressed in a long Snoopy nightgown. "I can still remember how nervous I was when I first came to Canby Hall. It was my very first time away from home, and I couldn't sleep for two weeks straight."

She grinned at Faith, who was busily stuffing extra film and a long-distance lens into her tote bag, along with her camera. "Then there was our visit to Faith's family in Washington, D.C. That was the second time. And now . . . Florida! It's like a dream." She drew her knees up to her chest and wrapped her arms around them. "It's not such a big deal to you, Dana, because you've been to Florida before."

Dana laughed. " I was five years old at the time, Shel. I'd hardly call it a peak experience." She snapped her suitcase shut. "This trip is going to be about a thousand percent better."

"Just one fly in the ointment, as my mother would say," Faith offered. She was on her hands and knees, digging out shoes from the closet floor. "And I think you know who I mean."

"Don't you mean two flies?" Dana said.

Faith finally found the shoes she was looking for, and held them up triumphantly. "Two flies," she agreed. "Pamela and Nicole."

"They won't bother us," Shelley said. "After all, they hang around with each other all the time. They won't have time to try to impress anybody else."

Dana smiled at her. Shelley was such an optimist. "I guess you're right. We can stay as far from them as possible, and concentrate on other things — like meeting boys and getting a tan," she added.

"Speaking of boys," Faith asked, "how did Randy and Tom take the news about the trip?"

"They'll live," Dana said tartly. "How about Johnny?"

Faith giggled. "He pledged undying love and that kind of thing. You'd think I was going on a trip around the world, instead of just a week in Florida. It's amazing what a little separation can do for a romance. He said he's already looking forward to the re-union."

"Boys are so dramatic," Dana said airily. "I think they're afraid that we're going to meet some fabulous guys in Florida and forget all about them." She grunted and swung the suitcase on the floor. "Come to think of it, that wouldn't be a bad idea at all." Even though she and Randy were more like good friends than anything else, she was still stung by his obvious fascination with Nicole.

"Well, I don't know about you two," Shelley said, tucking the covers up around her chin, "but I've done everything I'm going to do tonight." She checked the alarm. "Is six-thirty okay for everybody? That gives us forty-five minutes to get ready. We're supposed to get breakfast on the plane."

"That's fine for me," Dana said. "I'm going to turn in pretty soon anyway."

"Good idea," Faith said. She zipped her tote bag and yawned. "You know what Alison always says."

Dana and Shelley answered in unison. "Tomorrow will be here before you know it!"

"Know-it-alls," Faith muttered, and fell into bed.

CHAPTER TWELVE

I t's beautiful!" Shelley said ecstatically later the next afternoon when she got her first glimpse of the beach. She threw open the sliding glass doors of the oceanfront hotel room and stepped out onto the tiny patio. "I love it already!"

"Hey, how about a hand with the luggage?" Dana yelled. "I'm not a bellboy, you know." She was struggling in the door with two suitcases and a tote bag.

"I'm sorry," Shelley said quickly. "I saw the ocean and I guess I got carried away," she giggled. "Where's Faith?" she added, helping Dana drag the suitcases across the room.

"She's helping Alison pass out room keys, I think. She'll be here in a minute." She glanced at the two double beds. "Which do you want, the one by the window, or the one by —"

"There's been a slight change in plans," Faith said breathlessly from the doorway.

"We're short one room, so they're shifting people around. So be prepared. It looks like we've got an extra roommate."

Shelley turned around slowly. One look at Faith's tight expression told her what was coming. "Oh no, not Nicole. . . ."

"None other," Dana breathed, as Nicole strode in and plunked her suitcase on the bed.

"The stupid desk clerk got the reservations wrong," Nicole said irritably, not bothering to put on her famous French accent. She started peeling off her clothes, without bothering to unpack.

"What are you doing?" Shelley asked, startled.

"What does it look like?" Nicole laughed. "Haven't you seen anyone get changed before? I'm not going to go shopping in Florida in wool slacks." She opened her tote bag, and pulled out a tiny tank top and short-shorts.

"You're going shopping — now?" Shelley said. She looked helplessly at Faith and Dana. "But I thought that Michael and Alison want to meet everybody in the lobby so we can plan our afternoon. And we're not supposed to leave the hotel or the beach area without permission."

"Well, they'll just have to manage without me, won't they?" Nicole said nastily. "I'm heading for the shops." She wriggled her feet into a pair of straw espadrilles and started for the door.

"But what will we tell Alison?" Shelley said worriedly.

"Whatever you like," Nicole tossed over her shoulder.

"I don't believe it," Shelley said softly.

"I do," Dana said wryly. "C'mon, let's get changed and start our vacation. I'm ready to hit the beach, how about you two?"

"You're on," Faith said, and dove into her suitcase.

Fifteen minutes later they found Alison and Michael Frank surrounded by a group of laughing girls in the lobby. Michael, the guidance counselor at Canby Hall, was one of the most popular people on campus. Tall, with black, curly hair and ruggedly handsome features, he looked more like an actor than a staff member at a girl's boarding school. He and Alison had been dating for several months, and they were standing very close together, their hands almost touching.

Michael was smiling at the group of girls gathered around him. "Listen, you guys, I've got two announcements. First, we want you to have a good time, so please don't get sunburned. Save the lobsters for dinner." This was greeted by a chorus of laughter. "And speaking of dinner, let's meet at the restaurant next door at —" he consulted his watch — "seven sharp." He smiled and threw up his hands. "Until then, go to it, gang."

"They didn't even notice Nicole wasn't

there," Shelley said wonderingly. She was walking down to the beach with Dana and Faith, feeling very silly in last year's bathing suit. She'd have to get to the store and buy something new, she thought despairingly. The suit her mother had picked out for her in Pine Bluff was at least five years out of date, and it was so modest that she couldn't show off her new figure. And here she'd been exercising like a maniac for over a month!

"I guess it's hard to count heads when there are so many of us," Dana said. She was wearing a sleek, navy blue tank suit, and looked like a glamorous Olympic contender. "They'll miss her at dinner, if she doesn't show up, though." She put on a pair of oversized sunglasses and spread a towel on the sand.

"I hope for Alison's sake, she doesn't pull anything that crazy," Faith said feelingly. "Alison went out on a limb to take us on this trip, and I don't want sweet little Nicole to saw it off." She stretched out on a straw beach mat and gave a contented sigh. "Ah, this is the life," she said happily.

Dana nudged her with her big toe. "Hey, you're not just going to flake out, are you? Shel and I are going to go for a swim, or maybe take a walk along the beach."

Faith tipped her sun visor over her eyes. "A scouting expedition, huh?" she teased. "Well, I'll tell you what. I'll stay here and watch the towels, and you can give me a full report when you get back." She yawned and folded her arms over her chest.

"C'mon Shel," Dana said. "Don't get in any trouble," she teased Faith, who responded with a lazy wave of her hand.

"I can see why they call this place 'where the boys are,'" Shelley said a few minutes later. "It's just like the movie." She and Dana had headed for the more populated section of the beach, and were picking their way carefully over hundreds of suntanned bodies and beach towels. The sun was blisteringly hot, and the air was tinged with coconut-scented suntan oil. A gentle breeze ruffled the fronds on the palm trees, and rock music blasted from dozens of radios and tape players.

"So, it's just like you imagined?" Dana asked. She sidestepped neatly to avoid crashing into someone's cooler.

"Better. There's miles and miles of deep blue ocean and white sand, just like Alison said. And there's wall-to-wall guys," she added with a giggle.

"You noticed," Dana said wryly. "C'mon, let's walk down to the edge of the water." She took a step backwards and someone howled.

"Hey, you're supposed to walk on the sand, not the people."

"Sorry about that," Dana said coolly. She was all set to keep on walking, but a tall, good-looking boy about eighteen scrambled to his feet and blocked her path.

"I think I could forgive you." He had flashing dark eyes, a deep tan, and was grinning at her. "In fact, I think I'm in love."

Aggressive. But cute, Dana decided.

"Don't overdo it, Rick," his friend called from the towel. "You'll scare them off."

The boy called Rick took Dana's hand lightly in his own. "I read palms, you know," he said conversationally. "And this little line right here —" he turned her hand over and examined it closely — "says that we're destined to have dinner together tonight. Six o'clock at the Crow's Nest."

Dana had to laugh. "Is he always such a fast worker?" She said to the boy on the towel.

"That's because he's a New Yorker," he said, getting up and brushing some traces of sand off him. He had a flat, Midwestern accent, and a very bad sunburn. "They're always in a hurry." He smiled at Shelley. "They just don't take time to appreciate things, the way country folks like me do. I'm Terry Fielding" — he grinned to include his friend — "and this obnoxious guy is Rick Fulton."

"I'm Dana Morrison, and this is my friend, Shelley Hyde. Are you really from New York?" she asked Rick. "I live in Manhattan."

Rick laughed, still holding on to her hand. "I'm from New Jersey, but it's all the same to

Terry." He peered at her hand, pretending to frown. "So you're a New Yorker. Funny I missed that. I must be losing my touch."

"You never had it," Terry said wryly. He turned to Shelley. "Why don't you girls pull up a chunk of beach towel and join us?"

Shelley looked at Dana, who nodded. "Okay," she said, "but just for a few minutes. We want to take a swim before the sun goes in."

Terry winced. "I'd join you, but the salt water kills my sunburn. I went crazy the first day we were here and baked all day, didn't I, Rick?"

"He'd never seen the ocean before," Rick explained. "So he spent five hours on a raft soaking up the rays. Can you believe it? Of course, when you hear where he's from, you'll know why." He paused dramatically. "Iowa!" He laughed. "I didn't even know people *lived* there before I met Terry —"

"You're from Iowa?" Shelley squealed happily. "Me too!"

Rick smiled at Dana and shook his head. "Oh, no," he groaned. "Two of them!"

"Where are you from?" Shelley went on, ignoring him.

"Harpersville," Terry said, his face lighting up.

"I can't believe it. I'm from Pine Bluff!"

Terry nodded. "That's right down the road. We drive in to Pine Bluff to get ice cream."

"At the Green Hornet," Shelley said, pleased.

"Right!"

"Sounds exciting," Rick muttered, and winked at Dana. He edged a little closer to her on the blanket. "I think we've lost them," he said with a laugh. "Terry can put you to sleep talking about Iowa. He's better than Sominex."

Dana giggled. "Shelley's crazy over it, too. There's nobody else at Canby Hall from there and —"

"Canby Hall?" Rick said incredulously. "It sounds like something out of an English movie. One of those horror movies that always take place in creepy mansions on foggy nights. Is it anything like that?" He popped the tab on a soft drink and handed her one.

"No, it's nothing like that," she said. "It's a girls' boarding school in Massachusetts. But they did make a movie there, come to think of it, so you're partly right. A horror movie."

"What did I tell you? I'm psychic." He offered her a bag of potato chips and said thoughtfully, "Is it a high school or a college?"

Dana's heart sank. From the way he said it, she knew that he and Terry were college boys. "It's a high school," she said reluctantly. Now he'd probably think they were babies. "Where do you go to school?"

"Penn State." He reached out for a sweatshirt and held it up proudly "We're freshmen," he said, anticipating the next question. "So where are you staying?"

"The Sand Dunes. It's right down the beach."

"I know. It's a nice place." He laughed. "If you could see where we're staying, you'd die of shock. There's six of us staying in a really grungy one-room apartment." He took a swig of cola and stared at her. "But we party a lot, so we're never there, anyway. You know what I mean?"

"Oh, sure," she said, making an effort to sound casual. If he knew that Alison and Michael were along as chaperones, he'd really think they were infants. He was tracing some Greek letters in the sand, and she asked him about them.

"Phi Delta. Our fraternity," he said simply. "They're a great bunch of guys."

"It's starting to cloud over," Rick said suddenly, staring at the sky. "Want to get changed and meet us at the Crow's Nest?"

Dana hesitated. Rick was really an attractive guy, but Alison and Michael had made it clear that everyone was supposed to stick together. And there was that dinner at the cafeteria at seven. . . .

"I can't," she said reluctantly. "We've, uh . . . made other plans for tonight."

Rick's face fell, but then he grinned. "Sure, I understand. I shouldn't expect to get a date with a dynamite girl like you on a moment's notice."

Dana smiled to herself. He thought she had another date. Good, maybe he'd try again, she thought. "Will you be here tomorrow?"

"Right here," he said, patting the sand beside him. "If you don't find us, we'll find you."

There was a sharp crack of thunder somewhere in the distance and Shelley jumped up. "Hey, we better go before there's a storm. It's about ten minutes back to our hotel," she explained to Terry.

They said a hurried good-bye to the boys and half-ran all the way back to the Sand Dunes. There was no sign of Faith on the beach, but they spotted her in the hotel coffee shop. With a tall, handsome guy. They were sitting in a back booth smiling at each other over soft drinks.

"She certainly didn't waste any time," Dana said laughingly to Shelley. "I want to get a can of soda to bring up to our room. Do you want anything?"

"Just a hot shower," Shelley said. She dug in her tote bag. "I've got the key, so I'll go ahead."

As soon as she opened the door to the room, she knew that Nicole was back. There was lacy underwear scattered all over the floor, and the bed was strewn with shopping bags. The bathroom door was closed, and she could hear the shower running. She felt gritty and uncomfortable as she eased herself onto the flowered bedspread.

There was nothing to do but sit and wait. When Nicole finally emerged, pink and glowing, she strode by Shelley without a word. She dropped her towel and wriggled into a pair of tight white pants and a red halter top, while Shelley watched, fascinated.

"Is something wrong?" Nicole said coldly.

"No," Shelley said quickly. "I mean, is that what you're going to wear to dinner?"

"Bien sur."

"It's a little early for dinner. We're supposed to meet at —"

But Nicole was already headed for the door. "I'm not going to dinner with the group. Pamela and I have made other plans," she said abruptly.

Later, when she and Dana were sitting in the restaurant, Casey said sympathetically, "What a mix-up! I heard you're rooming with Nicole."

Dana nodded. "I wish you could have been the fourth in our room, Casey."

"Me, too," Casey said "I got stuck with Pamela and two girls I can't stand from Charles." She speared a crab leg, and said cheerfully. "At least we're spared their company tonight."

"What do you mean?" Shelley said, interested.

Casey shrugged. "Alison said that Nicole has a stomach ache and just wants to have some tea and toast in the room. Pamela volunteered to stay with her."

"Oh, so that's it," Dana said softly. So they had already lied to Alison. Birds of a feather!

The next morning, Shelley woke up early. The bright sunlight streamed in the window and cut a wide path across the bedspread. She could feel its warmth on her face, and she got up and padded to the bathroom. She vaguely remembered Nicole coming in late — it must have been around eleven — but there was no sign of her at the moment.

After she showered, she woke up Faith and Dana. "Rise and shine, and all that," she teased them. "Remember what Michael said — we're supposed to go to a dolphin show at ten sharp in Miami." Secretly, Shelley would have preferred to spend the day lazing on the beach — maybe looking for Rick and Terry — and hitting the shops. It was her second day in Fort Lauderdale, and she was still wearing her old bathing suit. It was maddening! Maybe she'd get a chance to go shopping after lunch.

But things didn't work out that way. The dolphin show was followed by lunch at a clam bar, a visit to an aquarium, then an alligator show, and dinner at a seafood restaurant. It was almost ten when the hotel van deposited them back at the Sand Dunes, and Alison warned the girls that she wanted them to turn in early. And still no chance to go shopping! Shelley was disgusted. Those stupid fish had spoiled everything.

"What a day! I never want to see another fish again in my life," she said feelingly to Dana. She was brushing her hair furiously, waiting for Nicole to finish one of her interminable showers. "I don't care how many hoops they jump through or if they can really talk," she went on. "In fact. I don't even care if they can read minds!"

"What's gotten into you?" Dana laughed, and Shelley glared at her. "Anyway, dolphins aren't fish. They're mammals, like us."

"Whatever," Shelley said irritably. The bathroom door finally opened, and she grabbed her shampoo and pushed past a surprised Nicole. A second later, the door slammed so hard it almost came off its hinges.

"I wonder what that was all about?" Faith muttered. "I've never seen her in such a rotten mood."

Nicole stared at the closed door and smiled. She was wearing baby doll pajamas trimmed in pale pink lace. "You Americans are so temperamental," she said with an irritating sigh. She grinned and got into bed.

CHAPTER THIRTEEN

"You've got a message," Alison said the next morning at breakfast. She handed Dana a folded sheet of hotel stationery with her name scribbled on the outside. "The desk clerk gave it to me this morning," she explained.

"I can't imagine —" Dana began, and then smiled when she read the note. "It's from Rick and Terry," she said to Shelley.

"Secret admirers? How touching," Pamela said sarcastically. She was wearing a white fishnet top over a pair of white linen pants, and stared coolly at Dana over her coffee cup.

"Not so secret, if they sign their names," Faith pointed out.

"A mash note, I suppose," Pamela went on. She saw Nicole's puzzled look and said dryly, "A mash note is a really corny kind of love letter. Something stupid and overdone."

"Thanks a lot," Dana muttered. "Sorry to prove you wrong, Pamela, but this happens to be an invitation to have lunch with a couple of great-looking guys."

She passed the note to Shelley, who was sitting across the table. "Can we go, Alison? We met these two boys on the beach" — she saw Alison look questioningly at Michael — "and they're really nice," she added hurriedly. She decided not to mention that they were college men. She didn't think it would make any difference, but she didn't want to take any chances.

Alison frowned. "Are they down here with a group?"

"Yes, they're students," Dana said quickly.

"One of them is even from Iowa," Shelley said eagerly.

"I don't know," Alison said. "I really think we should keep the group together, don't you, Michael?"

Dana saw Michael hesitate, and she said persuasively, "They invited us to have lunch right here at the coffee shop."

"I think that would be fine," Michael said firmly. Alison opened her mouth to object, and he laughed and held up his hand. "I don't think anything terrible will happen to them over a cheeseburger and fries," he told her. "You worry too much." He reached across the table and tapped her lightly on the hand.

"I guess it's all right then." Alison looked dubious. "But just lunch," she said firmly.

"We've got big plans for the rest of the day."
Pamela heaved a loud sigh, and Alison flushed.

"What do you have planned?" Shelley said,
trying to sound enthusiastic.

"Well, we're starting with a wax museum
in Miami this morning," Alison said brightly.
"And after lunch we're going to this fantastic
aquarium; it's one of the largest in the
world. . . ."

Another day of tourist attractions, Shelley
thought wearily. She tried to smile and listen
politely, but her spirits plummeted. Nothing
was turning out like she'd planned. She didn't
want to see any more dolphins or killer
whales. All she really wanted to do was buy a
new bathing suit and lounge around the
beach, but the weather wasn't cooperating.

She stared moodily out the coffee shop
window. It was humid and overcast, and they
were predicting thunderstorms for late afternoon. It made it rough on everybody, because
Alison and Michael felt that they had to spend
every moment coming up with new things to
do. Most of the kids would have been happy
to just wander around a shopping mall, she
thought, but no one wanted to hurt Alison's
feelings.

"The vans leave in fifteen minutes, everybody," Alison was saying cheerfully. "Let's
meet right out front."

She went to settle the bill with Michael, and
the moment she was gone, Pamela turned to

Nicole with a disgusted expression. "Can you believe it? Another crummy day! It's like a monsoon down here."

"I didn't think it would be like this," Nicole agreed.

"Me either. If I'd known it was going to be this bad, I would have suggested we stay in Yvonne's apartment in New York." She paused and turned to Shelley. "So you managed to pick up some guys already? A couple of fast operators," she said, and winked at Nicole.

"We didn't pick them up," Dana began.

"Of course not," Pamela said slyly. "They picked you up." She stood up and motioned to Nicole. "C'mon, I'll walk you to the lobby. I want to buy some aspirin out of the machine."

"You have a headache?" Nicole said.

Pamela laughed. "Not yet, but I'm working on it."

It wasn't until later that morning, when they were halfway through the wax museum that Dana realized that Pamela and Nicole were missing. They were walking through a dusty chamber of horrors when Casey spotted a guillotine and made a joke about Nicole.

"Where is she, ayway? And where's Pamela?" she said. She lowered her voice. "Not that I miss them, you understand. I'm just nosy."

"Weren't they in the van with you?" Dana

asked in surprise. "They weren't in ours."

Alison walked by then, saw what they were looking at, and shuddered. "I wish they could make these places a little more cheerful," she said weakly. "Why do they always have to concentrate on such grim things!"

"The Hall of Presidents was nice," Shelley said politely. "Very patriotic."

Dana smothered a laugh. "Except they all looked alike, did you notice? In fact, if you looked closely, you could see that Millard Fillmore and Lyndon Johnson were absolutely identical."

"You're right. The only difference was that President Johnson had a cowboy hat on," Faith offered. "But you have to admit, it did look sort of like him. . . ."

"And as for Fillmore," Alison said, "I guess they figure no one knows what he looked like anyway."

They rounded a corner and almost bumped into Michael, who had an amused expression on his face.

"What's so funny?", Alison asked.

"You're not going to believe this," he said, grinning from ear to ear, "but I just figured something out. Half the figures in here are identical! I swear, it's true," he said, grabbing Alison by the arm. "It's a gigantic rip-off. We walked through the Celebrity Circle, and it's amazing. Elvis Presley and President De-Gaulle could be identical twins. Elvis has a guitar, of course, and DeGaulle is wearing a few million medals, but that's it."

"You don't have to convince me," Alison said, laughing. "We just noticed the same thing. Do you suppose they get a discount if they buy them by the dozen?" She giggled and tucked her arm through his.

"Very possibly," he said seriously, and everyone cracked up. "Think how much money they must save. They can order a few dozen mannequins and then they'll have everybody from Richard Nixon to Elton John —"

"Don't forget Margaret Thatcher," Casey piped up.

"Good point. And Margaret Thatcher," he added. "All for one low price!" They walked quickly through the rest of the museum, laughing at some of the more bizarre figures, until Alison herded everyone back to the vans.

"What time were you supposed to meet your friends?" she asked Dana as the van careened down the highway.

"Twelve. Is that okay?"

Alison frowned and bit her lip. "I hope so. We're running a little late, and I hadn't thought there'd be so much traffic. You won't be more than a few minutes late, though," she said, brightening. "And after all," she teased, "good things are worth waiting for."

The sun made an unexpected appearance when they were about fifteen minutes away from the Sand Dunes, and everyone cheered.

"Do you want to cancel out on the aquarium this afternoon?" Alison said. "I'll leave it up to you. We can take a vote, if you want."

"You don't need a vote," Casey yelled from the back of the van. "It's time to work on our tans."

Everybody started clapping then, and Alison pretended to be disappointed. "Well, there goes my chance to be kissed by a killer whale. I'll just make the best of it, and lie around the pool, if that's okay with you."

"I can't figure out what happened," Dana said half an hour later. "We're not that late." She and Shelley were sitting in the coffee shop, sipping iced tea, making a tremendous effort to look casual.

"Do you think everyone knows we've been stood up?" Shelley said, glancing around.

"Not unless you advertise it," Dana said sharply. "And we haven't been stood up, you know. There could be some perfectly reasonable excuse why Rick and Terry aren't here."

"Yeah, like maybe they were attacked by a shark." Shelley finished her tea and reached for the bill. "This is silly. I think we should call it quits and join the rest of the gang next door."

"They've probably ordered lunch by now," Dana said, looking at her watch. I'll tell you what. If they don't show up in five more minutes, why don't we grab a sandwich and eat up in the room." She hesitated. "I don't particularly want to be seen sitting here alone, do you? People are going to ask questions."

Shelley nodded. "It's embarrassing."

"And puzzling," Dana frowned.

They were scurrying down the hall with two roast beef sandwiches when they saw Michael standing in front of their door.

"It's crazy," he said, scratching his head. "I was sure they'd be here, but no one answers."

"Who?" Dana said, reaching for her key.

"Nicole and Pamela."

"They weren't at the wax museum with us," Dana said, suddenly remembering. "I meant to ask Alison about it, and I got sidetracked."

"Pamela had a terrible headache. Too much sun the first day we were here, I guess. Anyway, Nicole offered to pass up the wax museum and stay with her."

"How generous of her," Dana said sarcastically. She pushed open the door, and as she expected, the room was empty. She stared at Michael. "She must have made a miraculous recovery. They're both gone."

"I guess so," Michael said, still puzzled. "Maybe they had lunch and went to the beach. That would explain it."

"It would explain a lot of things," Dana said with a meaningful look at Shelley.

Do you have a headache? Nicole had said.

Not yet, but I'm working on it, Pamela had replied.

"I better mention this to Alison," Michael said. "See you later, kids."

Dana shut the door carefully and sat on the bed. "I've suddenly lost my appetite," she said, putting the sandwich on the dresser. Well, this clears up the mystery of what happened to Rick and Terry, doesn't it?"

Shelley looked stricken. "You mean. . . ."

"I sure do." Dana sighed and glanced out the window. "Well, there's one way to find out. What do you say we hit the beach?"

Shelley hesitated. "Do we have time to go shopping first?" She asked.

"Shopping! Shelley, don't you want to find out what happened with the guys? We can go shopping *any*time."

"All right," Shelley said resignedly. She picked up her bathing suit and shook her head in disgust. It was just like that poem about the albatross they had read in English class. For some reason she'd never be free of the old bathing suit. She was destined to wear it *forever.*

CHAPTER FOURTEEN

Nicole was wearing the kind of bathing suit that could stop a college boy dead in his tracks at a hundred paces. *Her little shopping trip certainly paid off,* was Shelley's first thought when she spotted her.

Shelley and Dana had only been walking along the beach for a few minutes when Dana suddenly slowed her pace and whispered. "Two o'clock."

"Two o'clock?" Shelley glanced at her watch and frowned. It was barely one-fifteen. "That can't be right."

"No, silly. Two o'clock. Look straight ahead a little to the right," Dana said urgently. "It's them."

Shelley obediently looked and then gulped in surprise. Nicole was sprawled — gracefully — on a beach blanket, like someone doing a commercial for suntan oil. She was wearing the tiniest yellow bikini Shelley had ever seen, and her long hair was tossed over one shoulder. She'd pushed her aviator sunglasses up on top of her head, and had her face turned to the sun. She was obviously "posing," but it worked.

She looked fabulous.

Pamela was sitting next to her, wearing a sleek black tank suit that laced up the front. Her blonde hair was dazzling in the sunlight, and the French-cut suit made her legs look incredibly long and tanned.

"I can't believe they're not surrounded by a bunch of guys," Shelley said in a low voice. "They both look sensational."

"I know," Dana said grimly. "It's disgusting." She paused. "Let's go over and say hello."

"Are you serious?"

"Sure, why not?" Dana said, steering Shelley to the right. "I'd like to hear more about Pamela and her headache." *And I'd like to see if they say anything about Rick and Terry, she added to herself.* She was convinced that somehow they had snared them in the coffee shop.

Nicole had flipped over on her back when they reached her, and she and Pamela were giggling over something. They stopped talking immediately when they saw Dana.

"I heard you were sick," Dana said flatly.

"I recovered," Pamela said in a bored voice. "Is there a law against that?" She squinted against the sun, and put her sunglasses back on.

"Too sick to eat lunch, I suppose?" Dana went on.

Pamela and Nicole exchanged an amused look. "Actually," Pamela began, "we did manage to have a snack with some friends. Some new friends." She laughed, and reached for her lip gloss. "How nice of you to be concerned," she said sarcastically. "Great suit," she added to Shelley, who flushed. "Is that what they're wearing in Iowa this year?"

Dana was going to say something biting when she noticed the Penn State sweatshirt lying carelessly next to Nicole. And the cooler looked familiar, too. So they *had* picked up Rick and Terry! Her suspicions had been correct, after all. Casey was right. She always said that with Pamela, you should always expect the worst.

Pamela caught her looking at the sweatshirt, and said smoothly, "Was there something you wanted, Dana?"

"No," she said shortly. "Nothing at all. C'mon, Shel," she said tonelessly, "I think I'd like to try another section of the beach."

"Did you see the sweatshirt?" Shelley asked as soon as they were a few feet away. "Penn State! Do you think —"

Dana nodded. "I'm sure. It was the same cooler, too. Those rats!"

"Rick and Terry, or Pamela and Nicole?"

"All four." She stubbed her toe on a seashell and winced. "I wonder where the guys were? Probably in swimming, or buying drinks, or something."

"I'm glad we didn't run into them," Shelley said fervently.

"Why?" Dana looked at her in surprise.

"Oh, I don't know. It would be kind of embarrassing, wouldn't it?" They were walking at the edge of the water, heading north on the beach, away from the crowds. The air had a salty tang to it, and dozens of whitecaps were crashing against the shoreline.

"They're the ones who have the explaining to do," Dana said sharply. "I wonder what Pamela and Nicole told them about us. . . ."

"It doesn't really matter, does it?"

"No, I guess not," Dana agreed. "You know what we should do?" she said suddenly. "We should forget Pamela and Nicole, and Rick and Terry, and enjoy ourselves! After all, this is our dream vacation, right? Our once in a lifetime trip. Why should we waste our time chasing some guys who don't even matter?"

Shelley grinned. "You're absolutely right. We're in Fort Lauderdale, and we should be having a terrific time. What do you want to do?"

"Well, we can swim, or sail, or surf . . . but you know what I'd really like to do? Why don't we rent a couple of those rafts and ride the waves all afternoon? What do you say?"

"I say, you're on. Let's do it!"

"Where have you been all day?" Faith asked when they got back to the room at six-thirty. "I've been looking all over for you two." She was wriggling into a white cotton jumpsuit and her black hair was a cap of shiny curls.

"We've been on the rafts," Dana said. "What's up?" She shivered in the air-conditioned room and drew her towel around her.

"A whole busload of guys from some prep school in Georgia just checked in." She grinned. "And guess what? They invited everybody from Canby Hall group to a luau tonight. So if I were you, I'd get out of those wet suits, and into something great. You've only got half an hour. Everybody's going to meet down by the pool."

"A luau?" Shelley said excitedly. "Like in Hawaii? Hey, I knew things would start looking up."

Faith tied a red macrame belt around her waist and added a red bandana scarf. "What happened with Rick and Terry?"

"I guess you could say they . . . got lost on the beach," Shelley said with a little smile.

"You could say that," Dana giggled. "Anyway, who needs them? It sounds like we've got a whole busload of boys to choose from."

Faith fluffed up her hair with her fingers

and laughed. "You two sure are fickle." She pointed to the clock. "If you can get ready in twenty-six minutes we can all go together."

It took thirty-five minutes, but Shelley and Dana finally showered, dried their hair, and dashed out of the room after a very impatient Faith.

"All the good ones will be gone," she muttered.

The lobby was crowded with dozens of boys, and the girls hesitated, wondering what to do next. Suddenly a tall, brown-haired boy smiled at Shelley and put a lei of paper flowers around her neck.

"Canby Hall? I'm Jerry from Edgemont Prep and I want to welcome you to our luau," he said. "The drinks and food are right outside by the pool, and a rock band will be here any minute."

He reached down to get more leis for Faith and Dana, and Shelley whispered happily, "You know what? I think I'm enjoying it already!"

The evening was one of the most exciting that Shelley had ever known. She loved the way the patio around the pool was dotted with Tiki lamps, and the band played all her favorite songs.

She didn't see Dana for a couple of hours, as they had both been dancing nonstop. "These are the kinds of odds I like," Dana said with a grin when they met at the buffet table. "Two boys for every girl!"

Shelley met three boys, all named Bob, from Georgia; a really cute guy named Bill who lived on a ranch in Oklahoma; a Canadian who looked just like Rick Springfield; and after that, she lost track. She knew her friends were enjoying themselves, too. She saw Faith doing an impromptu break dancing demonstration at one point in the evening, and Dana seemed captivated by the captain of the Edgemont football team.

The party broke up at ten-thirty, but Dana, Faith, and Shelley lingered by the pool for a few minutes, talking to Alison.

"I just realized something. I've got three dates for lunch tomorrow," Shelley said in surprise.

Dana laughed. "I know what you mean. I made two separate dates for dinner. I just couldn't say no. They were all so cute!"

"You heard about the charter boat to Bimini the day after tomorrow, didn't you?" Faith said. "It leaves at nine, doesn't it, Alison?"

"That' right." She stifled a yawn. "I hate to break this up, gang, but maybe we should turn in. We've got a big day tomorrow."

"Yeah, just keeping all our dates straight is going to take some doing," Shelley agreed. "Tomorrow should be interesting."

"Tomorrow — hah! Tonight was interesting!" someone said angrily.

Alison and the girls turned to face a furious Pamela. Her voice was tight with rage, and she threw herself into a deck chair.

"In fact, it was more than interesting, it was unbelievable!"

"Pamela, you missed the party," Shelley began.

"What's wrong, Pamela? It's obvious that you're upset." Alison's voice was soft, calming, and Pamela turned to face her. Shelley was startled at the expression on her face — she looked angry, humiliated, almost on the verge of tears.

"I am upset!" Pamela blurted out. "And it's all because of that idiot Nicole."

"Nicole? What happened to Nicole?" Alison dropped into the seat next to Pamela. "Where is she, anyway?" She looked around as if she expected Nicole to materialize at any moment.

"Don't bother looking for her," Pamela sneered. "I left the little phony back in the restaurant. With no money," she gloated. "I hope they make her wash dishes."

"Maybe you better start at the beginning," Alison said. "Where exactly is Nicole? And what happened — did you two have a fight or something?"

"Something like that," Pamela admitted, calmer now. She glanced at Dana, a little embarrassed. "I . . . uh . . . took Nicole to a French restaurant for dinner tonight. I didn't feel like going to a luau with a bunch of jerks," she said defiantly, looking at Alison.

"Go on," Alison said firmly.

"Well, we had a nice dinner" — she licked her lips nervously — "and then when we had dessert, everything fell apart."

"What do you mean?" Faith asked.

"The chef came out from the kitchen to tell us about his specialty. He was from Paris," she went on. "I thought Nicole would be happy to meet him. He started talking to her in French, and . . . you're not going to believe this. She couldn't understand a word he said. Not a single word!"

"That's impossible," Dana insisted. "Nicole is French."

"So we thought," Pamela said nastily. "The little phony had us fooled all the time. She's American. I got the truth out of her. She's from . . . Kansas. Can you believe it! Kansas!"

"But I don't understand," Faith said slowly. "Why would she pretend to be French, if she —"

"Never mind," Alison cut in swiftly. "Pamela, where did you leave Nicole? I need the name of the restaurant."

For a moment, Dana thought that Pamela wasn't going to answer. Her mouth tightened, and finally she said in a low voice, "La Bonne Soupe, on west Las Olas Boulevard."

"How long ago?" Alison reached for her purse.

"An hour, maybe an hour and a quarter."

Alison made a little noise, almost a gasp, and turned to Dana. "I need someone to come with me. It may take two of us to find her, and Michael's gone for a walk on the beach. Would you —"

"Of course," Dana said. "I'll go call a cab." She scrambled to her feet and headed for the lobby.

"The rest of you stay right here and tell Michael what happened when he gets back," Alison said, her face serious. "We'll be back as soon as we can."

"Wow," Faith said softly when they left. "Nicole isn't even French! I can't believe it, can you?"

Shelley shook her head. "I can't. She had the accent — everything. Why would she do such a thing?" she said wonderingly. "I hope Alison finds her soon."

Pamela looked up and glared at them. "I hope she never finds her," she said flatly. "It would serve her right for making fools out of us."

CHAPTER FIFTEEN

She must still be in the restaurant, she just has to be," Alison said worriedly. She threw some dollars bills at the taxi driver, and sprinted into La Bonne Soupe with Dana beside her.

"Mademoiselle," a head waiter began.

Alison ignored him, and rushed ahead, scanning the empty tables.

"We stop serving in half an hour," he said pointedly to Dana.

"We don't want a table. We're looking for a girl," Dana told him. "Pretty, long brown hair —"

"Ah yes. She left without paying the bill," he said darkly. "About ten minutes after her friend."

"I'll settle the bill tomorrow. Please — which way did she go?" Maybe the pleading note in Alison's voice got to him, because he softened and tugged at his moustache.

"Who knows? There's not much around

here. Perhaps she went next door. There's a movie theater. . . ."

But Alison had already left, pulling Dana with her. She stationed Dana outside the theater, disappeared inside, and emerged minutes later, dragging a tearful Nicole behind her. Nicole's eyes were red-rimmed from crying and her eye-makeup was smudged. Dana was shocked at how awful she looked.

"You don't have to say anything until we get back to the hotel," Alison said, "but then I want you to tell me the whole story. Understood?" When Nicole nodded, Alison softened, and put her arm around her. "Whatever it is, we'll straighten it out," she said encouragingly. She handed Nicole a handkerchief and smiled. "Just hang in there for a few more minutes." She motioned for Dana to call a cab, and waited with Nicole under the theater marquee until it arrived.

The ride back to the hotel seemed endless, Dana thought. Nicole was wedged in the backseat between the two of them and never stopped sniffling. She glanced worriedly at Alison from time to time, and Dana, embarrassed, stared out the window.

Although Dana was outwardly calm, her mind was in a tailspin. What in the world had happened? And what did Pamela mean when she said Nicole wasn't French? It didn't make sense. It was obvious she was French, anyone could see that. If you couldn't tell from her clothes, you certainly could tell from her accent.

Of course, she tended to play up her accent whenever any cute boys were around, Dana admitted. When she was with Randy and Tom, she could barely speak English, but when she was with a bunch of girls in the dorm or the cafeteria, she managed very well. But that was just because she was a natural flirt, and she had quickly learned that boys were suckers for accents. Dana sighed. It was impossible to figure out what was going on.

When they got to the hotel, Alison found Pamela, Casey, Shelley, and Faith still at the pool.

"I found Michael on the beach," Casey offered. "He's in his room now, and he said he'll come down if you need him."

Alison shook her head. "I can handle this myself." She had her arm wrapped protectively around Nicole's shoulders. Shelley and Faith were trying hard not to stare at Nicole, but curiosity was written all over their faces. "How about if all of us go up to my room?" Alison said. "We need to talk this out." It was more a command than a suggestion, and everyone trotted up the stairs after her.

"I can hardly wait to hear this," Pamela said in a loud voice, and Nicole flushed.

"Shh, she'll hear you," Shelley whispered.

"So what?" Pamela said brusquely. "She can tell us all some more fairy tales about her mother, the countess. Or maybe the one about her yacht on the Riviera. I wouldn't mind hearing that one again, would you? It really gets better each time she tells it."

Alison turned and glared at her, and she responded with an innocent stare. No one said anything after that.

"You owe us an explanation," Alison said softly a few minutes later. Nicole sat on the edge of the bed, and the rest of the girls perched on armchairs scattered around the room. Nicole was silent, staring at her hands, as if she had never seen them before.

Nicole gave a little sigh, and said in a tiny voice, "It's all so complicated. I don't know where to start . . . how to make you understand. . . ." Her shoulders were slumped, and she looked tired and defeated.

Everyone was silent, waiting for her to begin. "Are you having trouble deciding where to start, Nicole?" Pamela's voice suddenly broke the silence. "And you can drop that little girl act, too. I'll tell you where to start. You're not French — start right there. In fact, why don't you tell them where you're really from?" Pamela gave a sharp bark of laughter.

"You want to hear the real killer, everybody?" Pamela looked around the room. "She's from Kansas, just like I told you before. Kansas! Isn't that right, Nicole?" she said mockingly.

Nicole bit her lip and looked up. "Yes, I'm from Kansas." She tilted her chin defiantly, but her lower lip trembled, and she looked as if she was ready to burst into tears. "My father's French, and my mother's American. I have citizenship in both countries, but . . . I've spent all my life in Kansas," she said in a faltering voice.

"You've never lived in France?" Shelley said in disbelief.

"I've never even been there." Nicole still was holding Alison's handkerchief, crunched up in a little ball. She raised it to her eyes and made a swipe at some tears that were trickling down her cheeks. "Pamela is right. I'm from Kansas."

Shelley could hardly take it in. She looked at Nicole's tear-stained face and shook her head. It was like some sort of crazy dream. "Pamela said you couldn't understand the waiter tonight," she said slowly. "What I can't understand is, why did you pretend to be French? We all believed you."

"Even me." Pamela's tone was bitter. "You've got a real talent for lying, don't you?"

"Honestly, Pamela," Shelley said disgustedly. "Why don't you just be quiet and give her a chance to answer? How can she explain anything if you keep yetlling at her?" She looked at Nicole and felt a rush of sympathy. "Go on, Nicole. The rest of us want to hear."

Nicole shot her a grateful glance. "It's hard to explain," she began.

"Well, give it a try," Pamela said nastily. "We'd all love to hear the truth for a change."

"Pamela —" Alison said warningly.

"No, that's all right." Nicole looked miserable. "She's right to be angry. You all are." She glanced around the room, and then out the window. It was a very still night, and they could hear the ocean in the distance.

"I've had a lot of trouble at home," she said slowly. "My parents and I don't get along very well. I don't even know why exactly" — she shook her head slowly — "except most of the time they treat me like I'm about twelve years old. I guess they can't believe I'm a teenager. They still think I'm a little kid."

"That's why you wore those clothes," Shelley said suddenly. "Those funny ruffly dresses and shoes."

"My mother picked them out." Nicole allowed herself a little smile. "No one in their right mind would buy something like that on her own."

Dana looked at her sympathetically, remembering the pinafore dress and patent leather shoes. She could imagine what it would be like to go to school in a get-up like that. She remembered how envious Nicole had looked when she said her mother was a buyer at a big department store, and was always sending her dynamite clothes. She had told Dana how lucky she was to have a mother like that. *No wonder!* Dana thought, realizing for the first time what Nicole must have been up against.

"You said you had problems at home," Alison prompted her. "Is that why your parents sent you to Canby Hall?"

"Yes," Nicole said softly, without looking up. "I was thrown out of a couple of schools, and they thought the discipline here would be good for me."

Shelley's eyes swung to Casey, who was watching Nicole intently. *She's probably thinking of all the problems she's had at home herself*, she thought.

"I jumped at the chance to go for another reason," Nicole went on. "It would be an escape for me. A chance to start all over." She turned to Casey. "Can you imagine what it's like to hate the way you are — to want to change every single little thing about yourself?"

"I can understand," Casey muttered. "I've been there myself."

"But you have to be French," Shelley said with a bewildered expression on her face. "I mean, you came to Canby Hall on a plane from France. Didn't you?"

"Well," Nicole began slowly, "that was all part of my elaborate scheme. I had two copies of application forms. My parents filled out one and I filled out the other — without them knowing about it. I made up everything about my background. Then, I offered to take the application forms to the post office, and on my way there, I substituted the one that I had filled out for theirs." She looked around the room at everyone's shocked faces. "I never expected it to work. I thought my parents would find out what I'd done and then get angry. I guess it was just one more silly trick I wanted to play on them. At least at first. But when no one found me out, I just decided to keep going." It suddenly seemed very important that she make them understand. "That's when I realized I could make a new life for myself at Canby Hall. I could become anything I wanted to be. I could be rich and beautiful and famous . . . like Pamela," she added. "Everyone would like me then."

Nobody said anything for a minute, and then Dana spoke up. "You certainly went about it in a funny way. Even if you wanted to invent some new personality for yourself, why did you have to go after our boyfriends? Why did that have to be part of the game?"

Nicole sighed. "I don't know. I didn't exactly plan that part of it. I didn't realize how the boys would react to that French accent," Nicole said. "They loved it. They ate it up," she said in a surprised tone. "And then once I started it . . . I had to keep it going. Don't you see that?"

"I think I've heard enough," Pamela said,

jumping to her feet. She shot a furious look at Nicole. "Listen, you little phony, you loved every minute of it, and don't pretend you didn't."

"But that's not true," Nicole cried. "I wished I had never started it. Everybody at school was so nice to me. . . ."

"And you figured we were all stupid enough to fall for your story," Pamela cut in sharply. "I can't believe everybody's sitting here listening to all this. What's wrong with you guys?" she said, looking around the room. "Don't you have the guts to tell her what a jerk she is? She's still putting you on! Doesn't anybody see that except me?" When nobody answered her, she stormed to the door. "Well, I've heard enough of your lousy stories, Nicole. I hope I never see you again!" She slammed the door behind her, and for a moment, no one said anything.

Then Nicole broke the silence. "She'll never understand," she said softly.

"No, but I think the rest of us do," Alison said. "It sounds like you were caught in a trap of your own making," Alison said. "You just dug yourself in too deep to get out."

Nicole nodded, and the room was very quiet. "And now what?" Alison went on. "What do you want to do — do you want to be Nicole, the French girl; or Nicole, the girl from Kansas? Do you want to stay at Canby Hall?"

"I don't know what to do," Nicole said in a little voice. "I guess the main thing is I'd like things to be different with my parents . . . make them see I'm not a baby, that I can pick out my own clothes, run my own life. As long as I'm away from them, it's okay, but once I'm home, it starts all over."

"That's because you never got things straight with them to begin with," Casey said flatly. "And you know what? You can't do it from Canby Hall. Look, Nicole, I don't usually give people advice, but I've been in the same kind of spot you're in. You need to go right back there and face them," Casey said. "Get everything out in the open. That's the only way."

"You may be right," Nicole said.

"I know I am." Casey looked around the room. "Everybody here knows that I was in some trouble last year. I made a lot of mistakes, but I learned something from them. You can't run away from your problems — they're right there waiting for you when you get back. And they're usually much worse by then."

Nicole nodded. "That's true. I was running away when I came to Canby Hall, but I didn't solve anything."

There was silence for a moment. Then Faith said, "Well, you got a better wardrobe." Everyone laughed and the tension was broken.

"But I didn't change the way I was inside,"

Nicole said simply. "Deep down, I was still little scared Nicole in the ruffly dresses." She paused and looked at Alison. "I've made up my mind, Alison. I want to do just what Casey said. I'd like to go back to school in Kansas —"

"At least spend the rest of the vacation with us," Shelley blurted out. *Why did I say that?* she wondered. Then it dawned on her. She hated the thought of Nicole leaving them when they were finally beginning to know her and understand her.

Nicole gave her a shy smile. "Okay, I will. I can't imagine why you want me to, though, after the way I've acted."

"Are you sure you want to leave Canby Hall? You don't have to, you know," Alison told her.

"No, I do have to," Nicole corrected her. "That's the only way to stop pretending, isn't it? It'll be good for me to spend some time with my parents. I think it's time for us to get to know one another."

Shelley got up and slowly walked over to Nicole. It was funny to think that if things had been different, they might have been close friends. She took a deep breath, and her eyes were suspiciously moist. "We'll still be your friends, Nicole," she said gently. "Whether you're in Kansas or Canby Hall. So make sure you stay in touch with us, okay? Because we really care what happens to you."

CHAPTER SIXTEEN

Everyone was asleep when Shelley slipped out of the room the next morning. It was barely eight o'clock, and she knew they'd sleep for another hour at least. She was finally going to go on her long-awaited mission: Operation Bathing Suit.

She let herself quietly out the door, and walked rapidly along the beach road. Alison had mentioned there were some nice boutiques there that opened at eight. With any luck, she could buy the suit and be back in the room by the time everyone woke up. What should she get? she mused. She'd seen so many terrific suits on the beach . . . some of those new vinyl tank suits. . . . French-cut maillots . . . and a really cute peppermint-striped bikini. Now that she had her "new figure," she could wear anything she wanted!

Moments later, she was poring over the racks of bathing suits. There was so much to choose from. She was torn between a baby-blue knit bikini, and a black one-piece with mesh cutouts. They both were fantastic. And there was a white lace bikini that would look great with a tan. . . .

"Why don't you take them all in with you?" the saleswoman suggested. "With your figure, I'm sure they'll all look wonderful on you."

So am I, Shelley nearly said. It was such a great feeling to go in a store, and know that you could wear anything they had. She thought of Cindy and all the hours of aerobics — it had all paid off. She'd have to tell her when they got back home.

She finally settled on a yellow shiny vinyl tank suit. It was different, exotic, not her usual style at all. In fact, she wasn't even sure if she could swim in it, but she didn't care. She was crazy over it, and nearly laughed out loud when she pictured the reaction of her roommates. It made her look wonderful, like she was all legs, with tiny hips and thighs.

At ten that morning, Shelley was alone in the hotel room, putting on the yellow vinyl suit. Everyone else had already gone down to the beach, and she had promised to join them in a few minutes. She thought idly of wearing a beach coat, and dramatically throwing it off, and then decided against it. *Let them drop dead from shock right away*, she giggled.

A few minutes later, she walked along the beach looking for her friends. The sun was very bright, and the ocean was a rich, cobalt blue. She felt like skipping, but forced herself to walk slowly, scanning the crowds.

"Oh, here you are," Dana said, coming up behind her. "I was afraid you wouldn't find us, because we moved our beach blanket out of the sun."

"Yeah, Casey was starting to burn," Faith volunteered. "We're on our way down to get some sno-cones; you want to come with us?"

Shelley smiled and waited. And waited. She felt her smile start to fade when no one said anything.

"Is something wrong?" Dana said pleasantly.

"No, nothing," Shelley answered, confused. *Yes, everything!* she felt like screaming. *Why didn't someone speak up? Surely they could see how terrific she looked!*

"Well, hurry up and make up your mind," Dana was saying, jumping from one foot to the other. "This sand is hot!"

Shelley stared at them in amazement. Maybe it was some kind of a joke. "I'd love to get a sno-cone," she said uncertainly.

"They're about a quarter mile down this way," Dana went on. "Why don't we walk at the edge of the water, and then we won't murder our feet?"

"Good idea," Faith agreed. "The water feels great today, doesn't it? Just the right temperature. Not too warm and not too —"

Suddenly Shelley had had enough. "Oh,

forget about the water!" Shelley blurted out. "What's wrong with you two?"

Dana was so surprised she stopped dead in her tracks. "What do you mean?"

"Don't you notice anything different about me?" Shelley said slowly.

"Different?" Faith studied her. "You've got more curl in your hair today, but it's probably the humidity."

"You're wearing that new charcoal eye shadow," Dana said approvingly. "I like it. It's very flattering."

"No, no, NO!" Shelley yelled. "Take a good look at me."

"Oh, you've got on a different bathing suit. Very nice," she said politely. "Is it new?"

"Of course it's new," Shelley said indignantly. "I practically had to kill myself to get into it, too. And no one even noticed," she wailed.

Dana stared at Faith and then back to Shelley. "Shelley, what in the world are you talking about?"

"I'm talking about my brand new body!"

"A brand new body?" Faith started to giggle, but stopped when she saw that Shelley was really serious.

"Yes. Look at how firm my thighs are," she said, grabbing Faith's hand. "You couldn't find an inch of fat on my midriff. Not an inch!"

Faith shot a helpless look at Dana. "Do

you know what she's talking about?"

"I'm talking about forty solid hours of aerobics, that's what!" She told them about the exercise class in Greenleaf. "I've actually resculptured my body. Cindy said so."

"Cindy?" Dana raised her eyebrow.

"My aerobics instructor."

"Shelley," Dana said patiently, "how did you happen to get involved in something like that?"

"It all started when I heard we were going to Florida. I wanted to get into a slinky new bathing suit — I've been waiting to buy one the whole time we've been here. I shouldn't even have bothered," she said reproachfully. She ran her hand sadly over the yellow vinyl suit. "My best friends didn't even notice!"

"Why was it so important to get a new one?" Dana asked.

"Don't you remember that awful thing I was wearing? I died a thousand deaths every time I put it on."

Faith laughed. "You looked fine in it, Shelley. I don't know what you're talking about."

"You really don't?"

"I don't either," Dana said. They were walking along the edge of the water, cooling their toes in the rippling waves. "I thought you looked great just the way you were."

"You did?"

Faith nodded. "Both of us did," she said firmly.

"But my hips and thighs are much thinner," Shelley told them. "And look — my waist is a couple of inches smaller, I just know it is."

"Well, if you say so, Shelley," Dana said absently.

"My triceps are really firm. Cindy said so," Shelley said, a little desperately. "And my calves — hard as a rock. Honest!"

"Right," Faith said, as if her mind was a million miles away.

This is unbelievable! Shelley thought. *If my body is totally resculptured, how come nobody noticed? If? Uh-oh, could Cindy have been less than honest with me?* she wondered.

After a few moments, Faith turned to Dana. "Do you want to try that seafood restaurant for lunch?"

Either that, or the Italian place," Dana said thoughtfully. "Maybe we should check with the boys first, and see what they want to do."

They walked along the beach, not noticing that Shelley had dropped back a few paces.

"Hey, you guys!" she said.

They turned and stared at her in surprise. "What's wrong, Shel?" Dana was smiling, but it was obvious that she wanted to get back to her discussion of restaurants with Faith.

Shelley stared at them for a long moment.

What did it matter if she had the skinniest thighs on the beach or not? Maybe the aerobics hadn't made as much difference as she thought . . . but who cared? She was in Florida, and she was all set to enjoy herself with her best friends in the whole world.

She grinned and ran to catch up. "Nothing's wrong," she said, linking arms with them. "In fact, everything's perfect. Now let's take a vote on that restaurant."

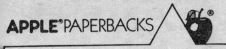